For ten years, Miles Farrington had known that his wife, Brenda, had been unfaithful to him. He had not done anything about it. He had not had affairs with other women. He devoted himself to business, to his hobbies and to philanthropy, and he tried to convince himself that he was leading a full life. But the time had come when he could no longer evade the issue.

His friends were telling him about Brenda's affair. She was being openly, boastfully, adulterous and Miles realized that he was a fool, not a saint, in the eyes of the world.

Something would have to be done. It would have to be something involving action, direct action . . .

"There's about everything the thrill reader could want in this *Room Service*."
—*The Birmingham News*

"modern and brutally frank"
—*The Boston Globe*

"This is not the type of book to have on the library table when the vestry meets in your home."
—*Buffalo Evening News*

"A short hard-boiled novel that is very readable . . . Mr. Williams has been at pains not to stack the cards at the end of his novel, and for that one admires him, even while being jarred at the final macabre note of the book."
—*The Saturday Review*

ROOM SERVICE
by
Alan Williams

Introduction by
Bill Pronzini

AN IMPRINT OF STARK HOUSE PRESS

ROOM SERVICE
Copyright ©1936 By Godwin Publishers
Published by Staccato Crime
An imprint of Stark House Press
1315 H Street
Eureka, CA 95501, USA
griffinskye3@sbcglobal.net
www.starkhousepress.com/staccato.php

All rights reserved under International and Pan-American Copyright Conventions.

ISBN: 979-8-88601-012-1
Staccato Crime: SC-007

All Staccato Crime titles are edited and produced
by David Rachels and Jeff Vorzimmer.
Book series design by *¡caliente!Design*, Austin, Texas

PUBLISHER'S NOTE:
This is a work of fiction. Names, characters, places and incidents are either the products of the author's imagination or used fictionally, and any resemblance to actual persons, living or dead, events or locales, is entirely coincidental.

Without limiting the rights under copyright reserved above, no part of this publication may be reproduced, stored, or introduced into a retrieval system or transmitted in any form or by any means (electronic, mechanical, photocopying, recording or otherwise) without the prior written permission of both the copyright owner and the above publisher of the book.

First Staccato Crime Edition: January 2023

New and Forthcoming Titles From Staccato Crime

SC-001	*Bodies Are Dust*	P. J. Wolfson
SC-002	*I Was a Bandit*	Eddie Guerin
SC-003	*Round Trip/Criss-Cross*	Don Tracy
SC-004	*Grimhaven*	Robert Joyce Tasker
SC-005	*Fully Dressed and in His Right Mind*	Michael Fessier
SC-006	*How to Commit a Murder*	Danny Ahearn
SC-007	*Room Service*	Alan Williams

Introduction
by Bill Pronzini

Alan Williams was born Louis William Lowenthal on June 13, 1890, in Washington, D.C., of Jewish immigrants from Germany. He seems to have been a very private person who never married, so little is known of his personal life and almost nothing about his childhood other than the fact that he had two much older sisters, Bertha and Cecilia.

The Lowenthals were a prosperous family. Father William owned a mattress factory, and their names appeared regularly in the society pages of Washington newspapers. Louis graduated from Washington's Business High School in 1906 at the age of 15, and in 1911 he applied for a clerical position with the Immigration Service. He was appointed to the Tucson office in the territory of Arizona, which would become the 48th State the following year.

During his tenure with the Immigration Service, he pursued a love of acting and writing in his spare time, appearing in numerous amateur productions around Tucson. By the end of January 1914, he had been promoted to Immigration Agent. Two months later he was promoted again, to Inspector in charge of the Phoenix office.

After several high-profile immigration cases, Louis came to the attention of Arizona Governor George Hunt, who made him his personal secretary in February of 1918. By then the United States was embroiled in the First World War. When it became clear that Louis would be drafted, Governor Hunt interceded on his behalf and he was commissioned as a captain in the Army, assigned to the governor as a military aide.

Governor Hunt decided not to seek reelection in 1918, and when he left office at the beginning of January 1919, Louis disappeared from Phoenix. Rumor had it that he'd left for New York City. When a letter arrived in Phoenix discharging him from service as of May 15, despite his not having appeared for a medical examination two weeks earlier, he was nowhere to be found. Louis Lowenthal had disappeared forever.

As Alan Williams, he surfaced in New York City's Greenwich Village in the 1920s and began writing and selling short stories to pulp magazines. Over the next 18 years, he published more than 200 stories, nearly half of them in *Breezy Stories*. Curiously, he also published one crime story as by L. W. Lowenthal, "The Greenwich Village Mystery," in *Top-Notch* in 1923.

Twentieth Century Fox bought the film rights to his story "The One-Woman Idea" in 1927 and adapted it for the studio's last silent film two years later. Williams moved to Hollywood in the 1930s, but instead of pursuing a writing career in the film industry, he opted to become a novelist. He wrote ten novels between 1934 and 1942, three of which appeared under the pseudonym of Peter Marsh. Most of these works were romances, some with femme fatale characters; his only crime novel other than *Room Service* was his last book, *The Devil's Daughter* (1942) as by Peter Marsh.

Room Service was originally published by William Godwin, Inc., a depression-era lending library publisher. Under the Godwin imprint, the company specialized in steamy (for the time) sex novels with provocative dust jacket art. In addition to these, their output included westerns and, in 1934, reprints of mysteries first published by the British pulp fiction house Wright & Brown. They also published a line of romances under their Arcadia House imprint.

While some of Godwin's sex novels contain criminal elements, only a handful can be classified as crime fiction. *Room Service* is the most accomplished and meaningful of those few.

Print runs of Godwin titles were small, invariably less than 2,500 copies per title. The vast majority were sold to small lending libraries, which held them for short periods before disposing of them in favor of new acquisitions. As a result, surviving copies are quite scarce. Only three copies of *Room Service* are known to exist today, and the novel has never before been reprinted—truly a Jazz Age "lost classic."

Publishers' dust jacket blurbs are notoriously hyperbolic and all too often unreliable, but Godwin's blurb for *Room Service* is remarkably adept and accurate. In just three paragraphs it sums up the novel's virtues, and is therefore well worth quoting in its entirety:

> "Room Service" is as concise and brutally frank as "The Postman Always Rings Twice." A Caspar Milquetoast is driven out of his home by an adulterous wife to find himself involved in a murder he didn't mean to commit and a wild flight from justice which carried him into sordid, degrading surroundings and which calls for the exercise of ingenuity and resourcefulness he never knew he possessed.
>
> It is impossible to adequately describe the tenseness, cumulative power and photographic realism of this novel. It is not a story of hotel life; nor is it a mystery, although it is motivated by murder; and certainly it is not a sex book, although the entanglements of the introvert, Miles Farrington, with three women are vivid

enough for any "scorcher."

We will not attempt to classify "Room Service," but we guarantee that if you begin it you will not put it down until you reach the last word.

The character-driven plot is deceptively simple. Miles Farrington, a successful New York City businessman, remains deeply in love with his cold-hearted wife, Brenda, despite her numerous adulterous affairs and her refusal to sleep with him. The breaking point in their relationship comes when she humiliates Miles in front of her current lover in their Park Avenue apartment, insisting on a divorce so she can marry the lover and then brazenly taking the man into her bedroom.

Devastated, Miles embarks on a drunken binge during which he picks up a young prostitute. He takes her to a cheap hotel, where in an alcohol-fueled rage he unintentionally murders her. Fear of police capture forces him to flee New York, to take steps to conceal his identity, and then to hide out in the slums of Philadelphia and Camden, New Jersey—a harrowing descent from Park Avenue to the gutter. Continual alcohol abuse, paranoia, and despair finally result in what amounts to a failed suicide attempt.

While convalescing in the hospital, the course of Miles' life changes dramatically. He meets Dot, the ex-mistress of a New York gangster, who is recovering from a botched abortion; he takes up with her after their release and renounces alcohol. When a surprise twist allows him to escape punishment for his crime of murder, he returns to New York with Dot and attempts to regain a semblance of his former life. What happens then leads to a darkly ironic climax.

Williams' lean, understated prose, while not quite as

brutally frank as Cain's in *The Postman Always Rings Twice*, is nonetheless perfectly suited to his subject matter. The "tenseness, cumulative power, and photographic realism" it evokes makes Miles Farrington's story unique and compelling. *Room Service* is indeed a novel that once begun, will not be put down until the last word is reached.

SCULPTURED LIKENESS—In front of books, which were a part of the stock at his shop on Wilcox Ave. near Selma Ave., stands a portrait-bust of Alan Williams, whose body was found Sunday in the surf at Long Beach. A former dramatic critic, playwright and author, Mr. Williams had a wide circle of friends in the fields of drama and literature, both in Hollywood and in New York City. Shown is Nik Jan Christian, sculptor who fashioned the bust.
—Citizen-News photo.

Despite the modest success of *Room Service*, Williams eventually gave up writing in the early 1940s and opened a bookshop on Wilcox Avenue, halfway between Sunset and Hollywood Boulevards and two doors down from *The Hollywood Citizen-News*. An article by Irving Hoffman in *The Hollywood Reporter* described both the bookstore and Williams' eccentricities and self-deprecating personality. One shelf in the shop carried a sign which read "Not Recommended." It was a shelf of his own books.

On Friday, November 2, 1945, after several years of ill health, Williams drowned in the surf off Long Beach, an apparent suicide. His body was shipped to his sisters, who were living in St. Paul, Minnesota. He is buried there in the Mount Zion Temple Cemetery.

One

For about ten years, Miles Farrington had known that his wife, Brenda, had been unfaithful to him. He had not done anything about it. He had not had affairs with other women. He devoted himself to business, to his hobbies and to philanthropy, and he tried to convince himself that he was leading a full life.

But the time had come when he could no longer evade the issue. His friends were telling him about Brenda's affair with Lester Nobel. She was being openly, boastfully, adulterous and Miles realized that he was a fool, not a saint, in the eyes of the world. In English novels the betrayed husband is a sympathetic charming figure. In 1935, in New York, he was an object of mirth and abuse. In the club, it was difficult for Miles to get into a contract game. Something would have to be done.

It would have to be something involving action, direct action. He couldn't talk to Brenda; he never had been able to talk to her. So he said he was going to Chicago on a business trip. He packed his bag (or rather the second maid packed it) and left the house, took a cab to the Grand Central; deposited his bag there in the check room, and then walked the streets for hours. He visited a few bars but not too many. He didn't want to be tight. Still, he knew he would need a certain amount of false courage, a certain amount of alcohol in his system to face them. The important thing was to decide the exact amount that was a certain amount. Finally, he decided he was just right. Anyway, he was sure he couldn't swallow another drink. He returned to the apartment. It was probably all a matter of imagination but he thought he noticed a peculiar expression in the eyes of the elevator man. He hated elevator men. He envied people who lived in walk-up buildings.

He felt completely sober. He should have had a few more drinks. Too late now. He was not going to face that elevator man again. He turned the key in the lock. Immediately Brenda called to him. Her voice came from her room, down the hallway. "Is that you, Miles?"

"Yes," he answered. There was not a trace of surprise or agitation in her voice. He enjoyed a few seconds of relief. The moment for action had not arrived. Then he noticed, on the ugly, authentic Tudor chair, a hat, a light-weight topcoat, and a pair of chamois gloves. Against the chair rested a handsome malacca walking-stick. He recognized these articles as the property of Lester Nobel.

But he could delay things a little by making sure. He picked up the hat and examined it. The initials "L. N." were cut into the sweat-band. Miles smiled triumphantly. He might have known that Lester Nobel would be guilty of such a vulgarity. He felt vindicated as a judge of character.

For a second he had forgotten the portent of these things so blatantly displayed in his hallway. Then he remembered. He put his hat, scarf and overcoat on the table, in friendly proximity to the more expensive furnishings of Lester Nobel. He walked down the long hall. Yes, he wished he had taken one or two more drinks. Brenda came to meet him, drawing on her negligee as she stepped out of her bedroom. She waited for him, making him walk the greater distance.

"Get that man out of here." He tried to make his voice impressive but, to him, it sounded very hollow. Brenda merely waited. "Get that man out of here," he repeated, "before I kill him."

Then Brenda laughed. "You'd better be careful," she said, "or I may not be able to keep Lester peaceful." Her voice was perfectly natural. That is, it was the voice she used in addressing him, dogs, and her small nieces and nephews. He felt as if he were a child again. His throat filled and his stomach seemed empty. As a little boy, he had always felt just that way when threatened with punishment.

Unable to say anything for the moment, he went into the library. Brenda followed him. She had to speak first.

"Only one thing surprises me," she said; "I thought you would bring a detective with you."

"How did you know I would return? How did you know I wasn't going to Chicago? I've never lied to you before."

"That was just the reason. You have no idea how obvious you were."

She took a cigarette from one of the boxes and Miles automatically snapped a lighter for her. Then he took a cigarette and lighted it.

"You planned the whole thing then? Have you no decency?"

She drew her negligee a little closer although she was fully aware that he was referring to her mental attitude. Brenda was coarse, lecherous, cruel and many other unpleasant things, but she was not stupid or ever lacking in subtlety of perception—although she was never subtle in her actions.

"You forced me to it," she said. "I've asked you for a divorce for five years."

"I hate divorce." His voice was firmer. His hatred of divorce had existed long before he knew that she was unfaithful to him. "You know how I hate divorce." He needed confirmation but Brenda said nothing; she merely smoked. "Why couldn't you be satisfied with the freedom I've given you?"

That was a question she was perfectly willing to answer. "Because I won't go on living with you. I'm in love with Lester and it's degrading to go on living with you."

"You've been in love with other men; I don't know how many during the past ten years."

"You mean you don't know how many I've had affairs with. Neither do I. But I've never been in love with them or said I was. Did I?"

"Not to me."

"Nor to anyone else. They were just an escape from you. Lester is the first man I've ever loved."

"You were in love with me when you married me." He knew immediately that he shouldn't have said that. It gave her an opportunity she welcomed.

"No," she said, "I never loved you."

It was foolish to continue this argument; sheer self-torture but he had to push on. "Then why did you marry me? You could have had plenty of other rich men—some richer than I."

"You don't really want to know, do you?"

"Yes, I do."

"All right. Take it then. There weren't many men anxious to *marry* me. Most of them knew me too well. Of the few men who did propose, or might have proposed, I knew you would be the easiest to handle."

"That's what you like to think now but it isn't true. There was nothing more perfect than the first year of our marriage."

"I was an actress. I kept right on with a boy I was having an affair with—"

"You're just saying that now."

"I'm not; that's why I wouldn't leave town for a honeymoon. For God's sake, Miles, don't let's go on with this. I may have been a nymphomaniac until I met Lester but I'm not an exhibitionist."

"That's just exactly what you are; that's what's driven me to this."

"I'd still rather go to Reno, but I'm going to be free and I don't give a damn what the scandal is."

"Why do you hate me so, Brenda? No one has ever hated me."

She did not reply immediately. But she did not deny that she hated him. "I suppose it's because you've kept on caring about me," she finally admitted. "Right now, if I send Lester away, you'll be perfectly willing to go on—"

"Not unless you swear—"

"For God's sake, Miles! I'm not going to swear to anything. Why haven't you kicked me out long ago? You're what the world calls a good man, and some women think you're handsome. They've told me so. Why do you bother with a bitch when the world is full of other women?"

"I don't want any other woman." His voice was patient as if he must still make her understand. "There is no other woman in the world for me."

"But that isn't human. That's why I hate you. You're not human."

"You want me to be an animal like yourself, is that it? You can only understand people who are depraved and cruel like beasts—"

He didn't finish. The door leading into the hallway was open. Lester Nobel came in. He wore heavy white silk pajamas with his initials, "L. N." embroidered in gold thread. On his pajamas as well as in his hat, Miles thought. Probably on his underwear, too.

He affected an Oxford accent. And Brenda said he was her first love. "Don't call Brenda names, Farrington," he drawled. "I don't like it and besides I've always hated to hear married people quarreling."

Miles made a supreme effort, although his impulse was to walk out of the room and out of the apartment. "You've got a hell of a nerve coming in here and telling me what you like. You're a—" It took him quite a while to think what Nobel was. Finally he had it. "You're a monogrammed rat."

Brenda laughed at that but Lester Nobel didn't smile. "Well a rat hasn't horns," he said. "Take off your coat, Farrington, if your blood is getting hot. You weigh as much as I do."

Miles felt the lump rising in his throat again and the emptiness in his stomach persisted. "You're a trained athlete," he said. "Brenda was first attracted to you when she saw you at Palm Beach last winter."

Lester Nobel looked at Brenda and grinned. She also smiled. "In other words you won't fight?" Nobel said.

"You're just a bully," Miles said.

There was a moment of silence. Miles struggled desperately for something to say but he knew it was not a time for mere words. It was a time for action.

Brenda finally lost patience. "There isn't going to be any fight or any filthy arguments," she said. "I just want one thing settled—how is the divorce to be arranged?"

"I suppose you expect a settlement or liberal alimony?" It was a question that should have been addressed to Brenda but, somehow, Miles found himself looking at Nobel as he spoke.

And Nobel accepted the question with a shrug of his silken shoulders. "That's up to Brenda and you. I'm able to take care of a wife but not, of course, in this style."

He indicated the room with a gesture which disarranged his pajama coat, revealing a body, lean and muscular, sun- or lamp-tanned almost to blackness. Miles was distressingly conscious of his own pallor and flabbiness.

"Put your clothes on and get out of here," he commanded and, to his own ears, at least, his voice sounded quite authoritative. He tried to heighten the effect by lighting a cigarette but he realized that was a mistake. His fingers trembled as he lifted the lighter.

Nobel looked at Brenda. She accepted the suggestion. "Not at all," she said, "Les' is staying; you're the one who is through here, Miles—forever. Fini. Remember this is my apartment; it's in my name. You took luggage to go to Chicago. Where is it? I'll have the rest of your things packed tomorrow and sent to the club." She waited. Miles did not say anything. "Or wherever you say," she amended. She, also, reached for a cigarette but they had emptied the box. She turned to Miles. "Let me have a cigarette, please," she requested.

He handed her his gold cigarette case, opening it as he passed it. She took two, handing one to Lester Nobel. Miles automatically snapped the lighter and offered it. Brenda accepted a light but, as Lester Nobel leaned over the flame, Miles threw the lighter on the floor. It broke. Brenda laughed. Lester Nobel picked up a box of matches from the table.

"I'm waiting for your decision," Brenda said. "Will you call in the elevator boy for a witness or shall I leave for Reno or Mexico tomorrow?"

"You'll wait until I make up my mind."

"No," she said very firmly. "I've been waiting five years. If I don't hear from you by tomorrow afternoon, I'm leaving for Reno and if you try to stop my divorce, I'll make you the laughingstock of New York."

"I'm that already. I'm not going out of this apartment tonight; I won't face the elevator boy and the doorman."

"Very well. It's up to you. I'm just trying to spare you. The walls are very thin between your room and mine."

"Terribly cheap construction—these Park Avenue buildings that were run up during the boom days," Lester Nobel said as if they were having a pleasant after-dinner conversation.

"Will you please get out of this room if you won't get out of the apartment," Miles said, "and let me talk to my wife alone for just a few minutes?"

Lester Nobel ignored him completely and again looked at Brenda for instructions.

She shook her head. "No. There is no point to it."

"I'm not going to use violence," Miles said.

"I'm not afraid of you, I'm afraid of myself. If you go soft as you always do, I don't know what I might do."

"I won't go soft and I won't try any further persuasion. I'd just like to clear up two or three things."

Nobel stifled a yawn. "Let's all have a drink," he suggested.

But Brenda dismissed that suggestion. "No. This whole business is disgusting. You forced me into it, Miles. For years I've been begging you to end this farce, decently and honorably, but you wouldn't. Now I'm all through and I don't want to prolong this another day or another minute. I don't enjoy it."

"You do," Miles shouted, suddenly finding himself almost in tears. "You enjoy every bit of it."

Lester Nobel stood up. "Come on, sweets," he said to Brenda, "if you don't want him beaten up, I'm not going to listen to him abuse you."

"All right," she agreed. "There's no sense to it; we'd just keep going around in circles all night." She looked steadily at Miles. "I want you to get out of here. It's my apartment—"

"Yes, you said that before—I'm not denying your legal possession."

"It's more than a legal possession. You get out of here or I'll call the night man and you'll find out—if you don't know already—whose orders he takes."

She took her lover's hand and they went out of the room without another word. They didn't close the door. Miles watched them go down the hall and into Brenda's room. They did not turn once. They closed the door and he heard Nobel's laugh ring out. If he had a revolver, he would kill them. He was sure of that but he had no revolver. The thought filled him with horror. More horror than he had known all night and it had been a night of horrors. He could never kill Brenda. He loved her. He always had loved her. He always would love her.

He burst into tears—violent tears of impotence and hysteria. He went into the pantry-bar and poured himself the stiffest sort of a drink. The sharp knife used for cutting limes and lemons dropped to the floor. He picked it up, examined it carefully to see if the edge were nicked and returned it to the shelf. It did not occur to him that it was a weapon just as deadly as a revolver, and much quieter.

He went back to the library, taking a second large drink with him. He walked over to the window. Fourteen floors below stretched Park Avenue, the red traffic lights reflected on the wet streets. It was raining. The lights changed to green as he watched; the endless stream of traffic started.

Red . . . green . . . red . . . green . . . red . . . green . . . red . . . green. . . .

He believed there was a two-minute interval between each change. Time seemed to pass very quickly as he clocked it with the lights. He must have been standing there fourteen minutes.

Red . . . on every red light, a taxi or two cheated and stole a block. Private cars were more obedient.

Green . . . eighteen minutes.

He opened the window. If he jumped, traffic would stop without the red light. For a few minutes anyway. Just for a few minutes. Traffic would stop but not the lights. And the police would start the traffic again. They wouldn't permit it to congest Park Avenue. The police were very efficient. Why didn't he telephone for a policeman and have his wife's lover thrown out of the apartment? A good, honest Irish cop wouldn't pay any attention to Brenda's claim that the apartment was in her name.

But there weren't many good Irish cops on Park Avenue any more. Miles remembered that someone (probably the doorman) had told him that the police department put their college men in the Park Avenue sector. A college cop might just sit down and argue the question with them. That would mean more talk. And undoubtedly Brenda was the more convincing talker.

He closed the window. It would be vulgar to jump and he might kill some innocent pedestrian. Or go through the top of an automobile, as had happened once when a girl leaped from a hotel window. He might crash through the top of a car belonging to some friends. It was just about the time for people to be returning from the opera. Many of his friends went to the opera. There were so many operas about faithless wives. It was, in fact, rather a trite subject and perhaps he was giving undue importance to it.

Perhaps. Anyway, his suicide at that moment would make it too easy for Brenda. He had willed everything he owned to her, with the exception of a few small bequests to charities. Brenda was also the beneficiary in all his insurance policies. Lester Nobel would be able to have his monogram in diamonds on platinum garters.

He could write a note but a note wouldn't be sufficient. He would have to make a new will and call the night men in to witness it. That wouldn't do. Brenda would destroy the new will and bribe the night men. And then the night men would blackmail her for years.

He had another drink from the pantry-bar; another stiff one. Then he went into the hallway and put on his coat and hat. He threw Lester Nobel's monogrammed hat to the floor. He didn't disturb the gloves or the stick or the coat. He opened the door and slammed it but didn't go out. He waited. There wasn't a sound. Then he heard laughter from the bedroom. First Brenda laughed, then Lester Nobel.

Miles opened the door again. He went out and closed the door very quietly. He signaled for the elevator and had to wait quite a while for it. The elevator man did not greet him. He hadn't even bothered to put his coat on. The Farrington apartment occupied the entire floor so no other tenant could have summoned him.

Miles tried to hand the man a dollar as he left the car but the heavy-eyed employee would not take it. "Thank you, Mr. Farrington," he said, "but Mrs. Farrington has given me my usual monthly tip. I'd rather not take anything more."

He slammed the door and took the car down into the cellar, leaving Miles standing there with a dollar bill in his hand.

He let himself out through the heavy doors. He turned up his overcoat collar and walked down the street in the rain. He hated the elevator man more than he hated Brenda or Lester Nobel.

Two

He seemed to be about the only pedestrian on that part of Park Avenue. Even the policemen stood in doorways or under awnings talking to doormen. And yet the rain was little more than a drizzle; to Miles it was cooling and almost comforting. He walked slowly, without any regard for crossings or lights.

An infuriated chauffeur, who had to throw on his brakes and almost skidded into the curb, leaned out to yell: "What's the matter? Are you tired of living?"

The answer must have astonished him. "Yes," Miles said.

He heard a woman say: "Drive on, Brooks. The man is drunk."

He wasn't drunk, he decided, but he wouldn't argue with the lady. Anyway, he was going to get drunk. He was going to get drunker than he had ever been in his life and he was going to stay drunk. He turned east on Fifty-first Street. Just as he reached Lexington Avenue, the drizzle changed to a downpour. He saw a few people running so he ran, too. They all ran into the subway station. He went in with them, put a nickel in the turnstile slot and waited for a train.

He rode two stations and then when he saw the numerals "33" on the posts, he sprang into action. He would have a drink at the Vanderbilt bar. "Make up your mind," the guard growled at him but held the door open.

After going through the turnstile, Miles walked to the left instead of to the right. That led him into the long corridor which tunnels under Thirty-third Street and leads into the large office building on Park Avenue. Miles was amazed to find this corridor filled with sleeping men and boys. There must have been fifty of them stretched out on newspapers, overcoats, and rags. Some had their shoes off, revealing filthy scraps of socks. Others were just a mass of clothing, their faces completely covered. Many of them were snoring lustily. One, awake, noticing Miles' interest and horror, petitioned for the price of a cup of coffee. Miles gave him a dollar. Instantly the place was a bedlam of begging, crowding men. Miles gave them every cent he had and almost had his overcoat torn off before he escaped up the stairs.

He had never encountered anything like it before. He had no idea such a thing existed. He didn't have any money now to buy a drink at the Vanderbilt and he doubted if he could cash a check there at that time of night. He could probably eventually identify himself but it would be an unnecessary bore. He took a taxi to a restaurant-bar on Fifty-second Street where he could always get money. The driver went in with him. Miles cashed a large check, bought the taxi-driver a drink, and paid him. Then, after a few more drinks, Miles asked that his money be changed into dollar bills. His pocket crammed with them, he went out into the rain again.

He went into the subway, getting off at every station. Wherever he found men sleeping, he awakened them and gave each one a dollar. Five times he went back to Fifty-second Street, had drinks and cashed checks. Each time he went into a different bar or club. He realized if he tried to cash the checks in the same place, the proprietor would think he was drunk and would attempt to talk him out of it. He did not feel in the mood for argument.

Finally, the alms-giving palled on him. For a little while it had made him forget. But after an hour or two, he was seeing Brenda's face instead of all the bums. And he was cold and wet and exhausted, and, perhaps, drunker than he realized. He went back to Fifty-second Street, had a double whiskey, and decided he would go to bed.

He cashed one more check. "Don't bother with a check, Mr. Farrington," the proprietor said, "just give me an I. O. U."

"No," Miles said firmly, "I want a check—and I only want fifty dollars. I'm going right to bed."

The proprietor, Charlie, elevated an eyebrow. "Does it cost you fifty dollars to go to bed? I can get you a harem for that."

Miles laughed heartily at the witticism. He wrote a wavering, ink-smeared check, pocketed the money, and finished his drink.

"Guess I'd better take a pint with me," he said, turning back to the bar.

"We can't sell it in bottles," Charlie said, "but I guess nobody can stop me giving a bottle to a friend."

Miles mumbled his thanks, took the bottle, and staggered out.

"Cab, sir?" the doorman asked.

"No," Miles said, giving the man a dollar, "I'm going to walk; need the air."

The doorman saluted. "Thank you, sir. You'll get water as well as air, sir. Good night, sir."

Miles tried to think what he had decided to do. Then he remembered. He was going to bed. But not going to bed with Brenda. Going to bed in a hotel. He wouldn't go to the club in the condition he was in. It was all right to get in that condition at the club but it was bad form to go there all toned up. He would need his bag that had been packed for the mythical trip to Chicago. He certainly hadn't expected to use it. He had checked it at the Grand Central. He thought he was heading for the Grand Central but actually he was walking west. Taxis pulled up to the curb but he waved them away. He zigzagged around corners. A cop good-naturedly suggested that he go home but made no effort to enforce his suggestion. A few panhandlers accosted him and were amazed to be rewarded with dollar bills.

He crossed Broadway but that did not arouse him from his reverie. He had forgotten entirely that his destination was the Grand Central. He was just walking, muttering to himself—a regular drunk in the eyes of the few stragglers.

Now he was trying to work himself into a frenzy that would stimulate him to go back to the apartment. Where could he buy a revolver at that hour of the night? Of course there were places. Maybe one of the bartenders in Fifty-second Street would supply him with a revolver. He doubted it. Money could do anything. But the bartenders on Fifty-second Street were not a poverty-stricken lot and would probably be afraid to take a chance. In some of the poorer sections, bartenders who did not know him might take a chance. He'd call a taxi and go to the Bowery.

But for the moment there was no taxi in sight. In the darkness of Forty-fourth Street, lined on both sides with theatres, a woman accosted him. She had to speak to him twice to make him aware of her presence. He was astonished. He thought that sort of thing didn't go on in New York any more.

"Mister," she asked, "can you tell me where the police station is?"

The unexpected question had a momentary sobering effect upon him. He looked at the woman with interest. She wasn't a woman at all; just a girl a very young girl, in fact. Barely more than a child. Pretty in a dull sort of way. Not the sort of prettiness he cared for. There was only one beauty for him—Brenda's. And she had never been more beautiful than tonight in that revealing negligee. But Brenda was home in bed with Lester Nobel and here was a bedraggled creature asking him the way to a police station.

"What did you say?" he asked, although he knew what she had said. Still, it seemed incredible. And somehow he wanted to hold on to her. And if he told her he had no idea where the police station was, that would end it. At least he supposed it would if her question had been an honest inquiry.

She put the question in a different form, displaying no impatience. "I think I'd better go to the police station; do you know where it is?"

"Hell, no," Miles said. "I don't know where the police station is. Why don't you ask a policeman? What do you want the police station for?"

"I want something to eat and a place to sleep," she explained without any hesitancy.

"How about coming with me and getting something to eat?" Miles suggested. "I guess I'm hungry—come to think of it. I didn't have any dinner and I've been drinking all night."

The girl did not hesitate. "All right," she said. "Thanks."

She walked silently by his side. Miles tried not to stagger but he was very drunk. They turned the corner into Eighth Avenue. It was bright with the lights of restaurants, hotels, bars, delicatessen shops, and other all-night spots.

Miles stopped in front of the first café they reached. "This one all right?" he asked.

"Sure," the girl agreed.

The place looked more like a public library than a restaurant. A great many people were sitting around, all engrossed in the morning papers. Miles and the girl found a table, clean and unoccupied.

A waiter appeared to take their order.

"What will you have?" Miles asked.

"Oh—anything," the girl said, "a sandwich."

"We need a good meal," Miles said, "not a sandwich. Shall I order for us?"

"Sure," the girl said.

"We'd better have some hot soup to start with." He turned to the waiter. "Do you have hot soup this time of night? We want some if you have it."

"Yeah," the waiter said. "Consommé wit' noodles or cream of lima bean?"

"The consommé," Miles said, "and then a good, thick steak for two. Medium—" He consulted his guest. "Is that all right for you?"

"I don't like it bloody," the girl said.

"Medium, well-done then," Miles amended. "Some hot, fried potatoes and some sliced tomatoes."

"Anything to drink?" the waiter suggested.

That reminded Miles he had a pint of whiskey with him. "Just a bottle of White Rock," he said, "some ice and glasses."

"I'd like some coffee," the girl said, timidly.

"Oh yes, coffee, of course," Miles agreed. "Wait a minute! Coffee will keep me awake; bring me some tea."

"Lemon or cream?"

"Lemon."

The waiter departed. The girl yawned. "Nothing could keep me awake tonight," she said.

Miles looked at her more closely. She seemed a little more alive in the warm restaurant. She was clean and not shabby although her clothes were very cheap and without any style. And she was hungry; there was no doubt about that to judge from the way she tackled the soup and bread. Miles discovered that he couldn't eat.

"Where's the White Rock?" he asked the waiter, irritably.

"Right away!"

Miles took the pint bottle from his pocket and opened it. The waiter reappeared with the White Rock, the glasses and ice.

"You'll have a drink, won't you?" Miles asked the girl.

"Is it whiskey?" she asked.

"Very good whiskey," Miles said.

"Just a very little," she said. "I've only tasted whiskey once or twice."

"Do you good on a night like this," Miles said. He poured a moderate drink for her and a large one for himself. He filled both glasses with White Rock.

The girl sipped the drink. "Doesn't taste very good, does it?" she said.

Miles looked at her steadily. It seemed incredible and yet he believed her. But it would be difficult to make other people believe that you could pick up a girl on Forty-fourth Street near Eighth Avenue at three o'clock in the morning and have her make a face over a glass of whiskey.

While they waited for the steak, she told him her story, although he quickly said she needn't tell him anything if she didn't want to. But apparently she was anxious to talk. She had come into New York on a bus from a small Pennsylvania town; she had run away from home and had expected to go to Philadelphia where she had cousins but then on an impulse she had decided to stay on the bus into New York.

The trip into New York had exhausted her money and she had hoped to stay in the bus station all night. But the bus people wouldn't permit that and had telephoned for some woman—Travelers' Aid or something like that. "But I slipped out before she could get there," the girl explained. "I was afraid she'd send me home or, at least, telegraph my old man."

"But the police will send you home," Miles pointed out.

"I thought of that when I was walking around," the girl said. "I won't tell them where I live. I have a girl friend in town I can reach tomorrow when she's working but I don't know where she lives. I think the police will let me talk to her. Don't you think they will?"

"I don't know," Miles said. "They'll probably make you tell who your parents are and where they are."

The steak arrived and she was silent until the waiter had served them and left.

"I don't want to go to the police," she said, "but I can't walk the streets all night. Won't you take me with you?"

Miles pushed his steak away. He couldn't eat. The girl was getting some color now and seemed quite a different person. She was young, and food and warmth and the few drops of whiskey had worked wonders.

"How old are you?" he asked. "You're just a kid—I bet you're not more than seventeen."

The girl laughed. "Thanks, mister, but I'll never see the 'teens again."

"You're a pretty kid," Miles said, refilling his glass, "no matter how old you are."

"I guess I'm not very pretty now," the girl admitted, "but I'll look better after I've had a bath and a haircomb and get some lipstick on."

"No," Miles said, "I like you better without lipstick. Where's your baggage?"

"I haven't any—I tell you I ran away. I had a row with my old man on the street; he told me to go home and then I saw the bus and decided to take it. He's beaten me for the last time."

"So you came to the big city! Well, what makes you think I'm the sort of man who runs around picking up little country girls?"

The girl gestured with her knife. "Don't fool yourself, mister," she said. "I'm no country dumbbell. It was all my boy friends that the old man was raising so much hell about. He'd just gotten wise that when I was supposed to be at my aunt's over Sunday I wasn't there at all."

"Where were you?" Miles asked. Not that he cared but the girl seemed to pause for a question.

She giggled. "At a hotel in Carbondale."

She told a few more intimate details of her stern home life in a coal-mining town in Pennsylvania and her escapades away from home with boy friends. These boy friends, apparently, covered a wide range in age and habitat. She had some coffee and a large slice of pie. Miles couldn't eat but had almost finished the pint of whiskey by the time her appetite was satisfied.

He paid the check, tipped the waiter very liberally, and they left the restaurant. The girl slipped her hand through his.

"How about it, mister? You're not going to ditch me now, are you?"

No one had ever called him *mister* before. It should have been offensively vulgar but he looked down at her indulgently. Cute little gamin. Her vulgarity was at least natural while Brenda's was acquired. And yet there was something about this waif that reminded him of Brenda although he couldn't for the life of him decide what it was. Certainly, there wasn't the slightest physical resemblance. Probably the quality of recklessness. He knew that Brenda had picked up men in public places.

"You must know some place?" she insisted when he did not answer.

"No," he said firmly, "I can't take you with me but I'll give you some money so you won't have to go to a police station. You can go to a hotel and get a room."

Her eyes filled with tears. "I'd be afraid to go to a hotel alone at this hour," she said.

"But you're willing to go with me and you've never seen me before in your life; don't you think you're a foolish little girl?"

"No," she said, "I'm not at all afraid of you."

Nobody was afraid of him. Not his wife, nor her lover, nor this runaway waif.

"You'd rather go with me than alone?" he asked, pulling out the few bills he had left.

"Sure I would." Her fingers tightened on his arm. "I like you. Take me with you, daddy. I hate to sleep alone. That's the reason I'm always getting in dutch, I suppose."

Her honesty was irresistible. "Okay," Miles said and felt exhilarated. Ordinarily he would have said *all right* but the spirit of the West Side street was upon him.

They went by taxicab to the Grand Central for his bag; then to one of the all-night spots back on Fifty-second Street for another bottle and a little more money. This bottle was secured, by purchase, from a waiter. Miles had the girl wait in a cab. He didn't want to take her into a place where he was known. That attended to, he directed the driver to one of the larger hotels in the Times Square district. He selected one, which he remembered was said to be owned and operated by a gangster-racketeer, one of those powerful crooks against whom nothing can ever be proven except, possibly, income tax evasion.

Miles had never been in the hotel. It was just a New York legend to him but so far as he could see, it did not differ much from any other Broadway hotel. In spite of the fact that it was not more than five or six years old, its rococo decorations were already a bit shabby. A registration card was courteously pushed over the counter to him. He had a momentary impulse to register as Mr. and Mrs. Lester Nobel but immediately rejected the idea and used Peter McCoy which had been his dissipating name back in college days.

No one seemed suspicious. Perhaps indifference covered the attitude of the hotel employees. His bag was elegantly respectable. It, in itself, was a suspicious circumstance since it didn't seem to belong with the bedraggled couple. Miles was drunk, wet and mud-spattered. The girl was almost obviously a vagrant. The clerk put them in a medium-priced room and made no attempt to overcharge them. He told them the price of the room but Miles, acting as he would in any hotel, made no effort to pay, and the clerk, with a quick, appraising glance at the bag, did not ask for cash in advance.

Up in the room, the bell-boy seemed astonished with a fifty-cent tip. Did they want anything to drink? Room service functioned all night. No; Miles thought they had enough to drink. Just ice-water. The boy showed them the circulating ice-water in the bathroom, checked the number of towels, and saluted good-night.

Miles was surprised to see that the room had a double-bed; he had thought, except for the use of one person, they had gone completely out of style. Probably they were reserved for couples registering after midnight in racketeer-owned hotels.

As soon as they were alone, the girl ran around examining all the furnishings and exclaiming with delight when she discovered the radio although it was disconnected at that hour of the morning. She went into the bathroom and Miles could hear her turning on the taps.

"I'm going to take a bath," she called, "I'm awfully dirty from that bus ride."

"Come here first," Miles commanded, "and kiss me."

She obeyed, somewhat to his astonishment. He was not accustomed to obedience when he made amorous demands. She had already removed her dress. She was a scrawny, under-developed little thing and seemed virginal to Miles in spite of her boasted affairs in the hotel at Carbondale. But he closed his eyes and gathered her into his arms with a drunken sigh of contentment. He had not even removed his coat. He embraced her wildly, insanely. This was the first woman he had touched, with the exception of Brenda, of course, since his marriage more than twelve years ago. He knew that Brenda had given herself to any number of men but that had not made any difference to him. With each infidelity he had taken more pleasure in his loyalty. Now he didn't care. Brenda . . . Brenda . . . you brought this about . . . Brenda. . . .

"What are you calling me?" the girl demanded, wriggling out of his crushing arms. "My name is Lucy."

"What was I calling you?"

"It sounded like 'bend her'."

"Excuse me," he apologized. "I'm drunk. What'd you say your name is?"

"Lucy."

"I've never known a girl named Lucy," he said. "It's a nice name; it's a nice old English name. All the girls in old English ballads are named Lucy; but they all die."

The girl didn't hear his sad reflections. She had managed to free herself from his embrace and was busy in the bathroom again. Miles was very drunk. He hadn't been so drunk in years. Not since collegiate days. He stooped over to take off his shoes but the effort made him dizzy. He fell back on the bed. The girl called from the bathroom. "Take off your clothes and get into bed while you're able," she suggested.

That was very good advice, Miles decided. He arose and opened his bag—his real leather bag which had been so carefully packed by the second maid for his trip to Chicago. Trip to hell!

"I'll lend you a pair of pajamas," he called.

"Okey-dokey," the girl accepted. "Bring them in."

He threw them in, discreetly turning his eyes. He was shocked by his reflection in the mirrored bathroom door. Brenda . . . Brenda . . . if you could see me now. You and your god-damned lover, now probably sound asleep, spent from your love-making and your laughter. Well, now I'm laughing and I'm full of vigor for love. Ha, ha, ha! I am laughing!

"What's the joke?" the girl called from the bathroom.

"I'll tell you when you come out."

"Okey-dokey. But you'd better pipe down. It's awful late."

But he would never tell her the joke. The only person he'd like to tell it to was Brenda and she'd never listen. He took off his coat, his waistcoat, and his other shoe. Then he fell back on the bed.

Someone was shaking him. He leaped to his feet. "What the hell!"

She laughed. "Wake up, big boy." His pajamas were folded and belted around her and turned up with cuffs reaching almost to her knees. She looked more childlike than ever. Her hair was tied in a turkish towel.

"I never saw so many towels," she said. "Believe me, in Carbondale you get two."

"Let's have a drink," Miles suggested.

"Okey-dokey," she agreed.

"I'll telephone room service for some ice-water and ginger-ale. Which'd you rather have."

She reminded him of the running ice-water in the bathroom.

"That'll do," Miles agreed.

"I'll get it," she volunteered as he staggered to his feet.

He fell back on the bed and removed more of his clothing. The girl brought him the drink and he raised it to his lips. But he couldn't drink any more; it was physically impossible. The girl was sipping hers with more enjoyment than she had shown in the restaurant.

He fell back on the bed again. "Let me help you," the girl said. But he sat up quickly when she pulled off one of his socks.

"Don't do that," he said with dignity; "you get into bed and I'll turn out the light."

"Okey-dokey," she said and obeyed. Miles switched out the lights and undressed in the dark, letting his clothes fall to the floor, something he had never done in his well-ordered life.

"Gosh," he muttered, "the room keeps going round and around. I guess I'm tight all right, honey . . . what's your name—Elaine?"

"No, Lucy. And you'd better get into bed before you fall down."

"You said that before but you're right." He sat down on the edge of the bed and then slipped under the covers. She was there. "I'm glad you're here with me, Lucy."

"Okey-dokey. Gee, these pajamas are some fit. Will you buy me some clothes in the morning, daddy?"

That brought him back to reality. His mind was fairly clear. Only his muscles had ceased functioning. What had he let himself in for? She was assuming a relationship that would extend beyond the night. He would soon get that idea out of her stupid little head.

"I'm leaving town in the morning," he said; "that's why I had my bag packed at the station. I am going to Chicago."

"Will you take me with you?"

She put her arm around him but he threw it off. "No, I won't take you with me."

She began to cry. "You think I'm just a little street tart, that's what you think, I know you do."

Miles put his arms around her and found her pleasantly comforting. "Don't cry," he said. "I don't think any such thing. Don't forget I just brought you here because you asked me to—and it's better than the police station, isn't it?"

"I don't know whether it is or not. You're hurting me; don't you play too rough. You've probably got a wife and a family. You're going back to them tomorrow . . . that's where you're going. And where'll I be? Trying to find a job in New York. I know puh-lenty about men—even if I do come from a hick town."

"I'm not going to my wife . . . she's going to Reno. I'll take you to the apartment and give you all the clothes she leaves behind."

The girl tried to pull out of his arms but he would not release her. "What do you think I am?" she demanded indignantly. "I don't want your wife's cast-off clothing. Aren't you going to be nice to me, daddy? And don't you hurt me. Gee, what do you think I am?"

Miles wondered if he ought to tell her. "I don't know what you are," he growled. God, how he hated a whining woman. Brenda had never whined.

The girl in bed with him kept blubbering. Was there no way of shutting her up? Suddenly she started to cry and when he ignored that she became hysterical.

"If you keep still," he said, "I'll buy you all the clothes you want in the morning."

She was quiet immediately; that is, she stopped weeping—but not talking. "Okey-dokey," she said, "but don't think you can buy me off with a few dresses. What'll I do ... what'll I do when my folks find out about this? My father'll kill me ... how do I know what'll happen to me? It's easy for you ... but suppose'n I have to have an operation? You'll buy me a dress ... if you eat regular you'll—"

Miles put his hand over her mouth. "Shut up!" he said.

She was frightened into silence for a moment. He reached out for the light and knocked the bedside table over.

"What are you doing?" the girl asked.

"Trying to find a drink."

She got out of bed, turned on the light and found that the whiskey bottle was undamaged. Miles almost snatched it out of her hand and took a long drink from it, not bothering with a glass.

"You might have the politeness to offer me one," the girl said, wiping her tears away with the corner of the pillow case.

"Help yourself," Miles said, falling back on the bed.

"Okey-dokey," she said, pouring the whiskey from the bottle into the glass and going into the bathroom for ice-water.

Miles sat up in bed. "Stop saying that!" he screamed.

She appeared in the doorway from the bathroom, drinking and crying. "Stop saying what?"

"Okey-dokey."

"Okey-dokey, I won't say it any more."

She picked up the table, arranged it, picked up Miles' trousers, turned out the light but did not get into bed immediately. Miles was sure she was going through his pockets. He didn't give a damn. She was welcome to what she found. He pretended to be asleep.

She got into bed and put her head on his shoulder.

"Daddy!" she whispered. He did not answer. She repeated the endearment with a whimper.

"What is it?" Miles muttered.

"Won't you take me with you where you're going?"

"No."

She began to sob again, at first, quietly, and then when Miles ignored her, more wildly.

"You've just got on a crying jag," he said, unsympathetically. "Go to sleep."

To his surprise, she was suddenly quiet. Could she have fallen asleep that quickly? God, how disgusting it was to have her there next to him, her wet face on his shoulder.

He had a sudden idea that he would call Brenda on the telephone and tell her he was in bed with another woman; he'd let Brenda listen to the girl breathe. Or if she didn't believe him, he'd wake the girl up and make her talk to Brenda. He shook the girl roughly.

"What do you want?" she asked sleepily. "I'm tired."

"I want you to talk to my wife," Miles said. "I'm going to talk to her on the telephone."

"You're nerts," the girl said. "Have another drink and go to sleep."

"All right," Miles agreed. He found the bottle in the darkness instead of the telephone. He took a drink.

"Keep the bottle in bed with you," the girl suggested. "Then you won't be knocking over things and stepping on my stomach."

Miles put the bottle under his pillow. "All right," he said, "let's go to sleep."

"Okey-dokey."

He slapped her across the mouth. That was the way he should have slapped Brenda earlier in the evening. "I told you not to say that."

"I'll say what I feel like ... don't you dast hit me, you son of a bitch ... stop it, you're hurting me ... I've a great mind to call downstairs and tell them to send up a cop. And I thought you was a gent'man."

Miles turned away from her. "Brenda, Brenda ..." he sobbed.

"My name's Lucy, I told you, and if you can't call me that, don't call me nothing. I don't like to be called other women's names."

"For Christ's sake," Miles implored, "keep still, will you, before I go crazy."

"I don't care what you do. I won't shut up ... you can't make me shut up—my own father couldn't make me shut up and you're not half the man that he was ... you cheap bastard ... take your fingers off'n my throat will you? You're hurting me ... take your fingers off my throat!"

She wriggled out of his grasp but didn't have sense enough to keep still. "I ought to telephone downstairs and tell them to send a policeman up here ... that's what I ought to do and, believe me, pal, if you don't treat me right in the morning ..."

He hated her. He hated her body next to his. Brenda had never slept in the same bed with him. Not even on their honeymoon. Now for years, she had been occupying a room alone. But she had a double bed in it.

"Are you listening to me? Are you going to be nice to me in the morning, daddy? Are you going to be nice to me until I get a job?"

"I'm telling you to shut up," Miles said doggedly, "or I'll hit you so hard, you will be still."

"Oh yeah; just try it. Just hit me once more . . . just once more . . . I bet you won't hit anybody else for a long time . . . I don't take it from nobody . . . I ran away so the old man wouldn't hit me any more and why should I take it from you . . . a stranger. You guessed right the first time, you four-flusher, but you didn't have sense enough to follow your hunch . . . I'm jail-bait, mister, that's what I am; seventeen is the age and that ain't so okey-dokey, is it?"

He hit her as hard as he could with his open palm and then before she could make another sound, he threw the pillow over her face and pressed down on it. He had strength; maybe not so much as that polo-boy, Lester Nobel, but he had strength. Her body twisted around violently. Her whining and then her screams were muffled in the pillow. He threw himself on her. He held her down with the main force of his body. He was intoxicated with more than whiskey; he was intoxicated by his own strength and power. His blood was up in the true meaning of the words. He felt it pounding through his veins. He was master of this woman. He'd keep her still; he could feel her writhing under him; trying, desperately, to free herself. Helpless. This was the way he should have treated Brenda when she had taunted him with his weakness. He should have mastered her this way . . . it was entirely possible to close his eyes and think it was Brenda . . . and it was Brenda. . . .

Now she was quiet . . . completely quiet . . . this woman who wasn't Brenda and yet was Brenda. Now he could sleep. He was suddenly very tired; completely exhausted and completely relaxed. He didn't want any more liquor. He just wanted to rest. He turned on his side and slept. And the girl was quiet, too.

Three

For hours he lay there asleep in a state of complete intoxication and exhaustion. He breathed heavily and slept without moving or dreaming. Daylight came but it did not disturb him. The morning noises of the hotel did not disturb him. Hours passed and his sleep was not quite so heavy. He began to dream.

He and Brenda were driving—faster and faster. Brenda kept urging him on—faster and faster. It began to get very cold. The ice was forming thick around them. It coated the windshield. He asked Brenda if she weren't cold but she told him to drive faster. He was almost awake and drew the cover up over him but the cold continued and he dreamed again. But now he was alone; Brenda was out of his dream.

Someone knocked at the door but it did not awaken him immediately. He dreamed that they were trying to break up the ice and release him. They were pounding on it. The maid inserted her pass-key in the lock and opened the door a few inches. She saw the couple on the bed—or the outline of a couple—and quickly closed the door with a muttered, half-hearted apology. "I'm just checking up on the rooms; I won't disturb you."

The voice brought him out of his dream but not to full consciousness. He had no idea where he was. He knew, vaguely, that he was not in his own bed. Then he realized that the coldness was in the bed with him. He turned over, pulled back the covers and then leaped out of the bed. There was a sort of rattle in his throat but he made no audible outcry.

Memory returned slowly and in fragments. It was a blurred memory as if the thing had happened years before. He saw the pint bottle of whiskey which had slipped down from beneath the pillow. That was probably part of his icy dream, also. Maybe . . . but no, even an unprofessional examination revealed that the girl had been dead for hours.

He held the bottle to his lips and took a drink; there wasn't very much. He had never been a morning drinker but somehow it tasted good. And warmed him. That damnable cold—he could still feel it. He remembered the details—most of them. So he had suffocated her with the pillow. The Othello-Desdemona business was possible then and not merely a thing of poetic imagination. How had he managed to keep her still while he suffocated her? Then he remembered that he had held her down with the force of his body.

The amazing thing to him was that the recollection did not fill him with horror. It seemed completely impersonal. He wasn't actually sorry. This miserable creature's life wasn't worth anything. A cheap, young-looking whore with a line about coming from the country. The pillow had fallen away from her face. It was rather a dreadful sight and he threw a towel over it. He remembered that she had been amazed by the generosity of the hotel in furnishing towels.

He picked up the telephone and then he put it down again. Excitement was still in his blood and he remembered about Brenda and her lover. Let the police catch him. They would, of course, in time, but in the meantime he could stay drunk and enjoy it. His last drunk. His first and last, really. Of course, he had been drunk before but never from one day to another. That, to him, was always the sign of a real drunk—the mark of the alcoholic. Well, he wasn't alcoholic but he'd stay drunk until they caught him.

Brenda would be in the limelight. How she would loathe that. The night men at the apartment would all be interviewed and maybe they would tell the truth. He chuckled quietly as he took another drink from the bottle. It was almost empty. He'd have to get more. In the meantime he realized that he must do a little clear thinking even to get out of the hotel. It wouldn't be sporting to be caught right in the room with the body. A cold shower, he decided, was the thing most necessary at the moment.

Suddenly he remembered that someone had been at the door. Someone had opened it and spoken to him. Were they waiting for him outside? Were they afraid to open the door, thinking he might be armed and desperate? He opened the door a few inches. No one was in sight. He closed the door. It had a snap lock and there was no way of guarding against it being opened from the outside with a pass-key. Yes, there was. He found a little push-bolt which would give complete security from intrusion. That was probably the advantage of committing a murder in a gangster hotel.

Then he went back to the bathroom. The thing was quite exhilarating. He hadn't felt so on his toes since he first went into business after graduating from college. Miles Farrington a murderer! He examined himself in the mirrored door of the bathroom. Of course, he looked rather drawn and bloodshot after a night of drinking but, otherwise, he couldn't see any change—any haunted expression. He didn't feel haunted. He was sure the general public would be surprised when he was proclaimed a murderer. That blue-eyed, sandy-haired guy! But he was getting a paunch. He went through a few listless exercises and then suddenly realized it was a poor time to be taking off weight.

And when Brenda heard the news, she would know what a narrow escape she had. The thought of Brenda brought no pain or humiliation. That was done with. The whole quarrel seemed petty and unimportant. Let her marry her polo-boy. Her husband was a murderer. He had killed a man. Not a man in the strict sense of gender but a fellowman. A human being.

He looked at his wrist watch which he was still wearing. Twenty after twelve. He must have slept about eight hours. Good! He was a man who needed his eight hours. He stripped and took a hot and then a cold shower; he shaved and dressed, carefully, putting on clean linen. The telephone rang. Who on earth could be calling him? No one knew he was there. He had registered under a phony name. What name had he used? For the life of him, he couldn't remember that.

It rang again. If he did not answer, they would certainly come up. He answered. It was Room Service, wanting to know if Mr. and Mrs. McCoy would care to have breakfast served in their room. "There is no extra charge for the service," the voice cooed.

Mr. McCoy thanked Room Service but he did not care for breakfast just yet. Maybe a little later. . . .

Well, that was a help. McCoy. Peter McCoy, of course. His college name when they made the rounds.

He packed his bag, checking and rechecking to make sure that he had not forgotten anything. Then he forced himself to look at the girl on the bed. He could not see any marks on her throat. A very clean case of suffocation. How would the doctor know she had been choked and suffocated. But, apparently, judging by detective stories, doctors were able to determine such things very quickly and accurately.

She was wearing his pajamas. That was almost the one thing—the inevitable one thing—that he had overlooked. He would have to remove them. If he had forgotten them, he would have been identified within a very short time by the laundry mark. But his things were never sent to a laundry; Brenda had them done at home.

And the pajamas, he recalled, as he pulled them from the emaciated, cold body had been purchased from their maker in China. It would have been quite difficult at that. They probably would have suspected a Japanese spy.

He searched the bed very carefully for a stray handkerchief. Nothing. Of course, he was forgetting one thing; murderers always do but he'd be damned if he could find it. The empty whiskey bottle! That might be traced to the Fifty-second Street saloon. He packed the empty bottle. Of course, his fingerprints were on everything but his fingerprints weren't registered. John D. Rockefeller, jr., had been fingerprinted as an example to his fellow citizens but Miles hadn't taken the hint. He doubted very much if John D., jr., would be suspected.

He closed his bag again and sat down to think for a minute before leaving. The only immediate danger as he saw it was that the body would be discovered before he left the hotel. He placed the "Do Not Disturb" sign on the doorknob. In the corridor he met the maid. He tipped her fifty cents and told her his wife wanted to sleep for several more hours. That, he decided, as he stepped into the elevator, was foolish move number one. The sign on the door would have been enough. There had been a murder play once by that title——"The Sign on the Door." Now the maid had taken a good look at him, would remember the fifty cent tip which was probably excessive, and would be able to make an identification.

He paid his bill which almost exhausted his money and explained to the cashier that his wife would be in the room for awhile. The cashier assured him that she would not be disturbed until six o'clock. A bell-boy took his bag and deposited it in a taxicab.

He drove to the Grand Central and then, realizing that the bell-boy and the taxi-driver would both remember his destination, he walked through the station, took another taxi and went to the Pennsylvania Station where he checked the bag in the parcel room. That, he decided, was very clever.

He would need money. He must get to the bank before the alarm was raised. He had no idea how much money he had drawn the night before but he was sure his bank balance was ample and if it weren't the bank would take care of an over-draft. He stopped at the Pennsylvania Hotel bar for several drinks. He was positive he saw no one he knew.

At the bank, he drew five hundred dollars. Any more, he felt, would arouse suspicion. As it was, the teller looked at him curiously. He wondered why. Five hundred dollars was not such a large amount; of course, it was more than he usually drew. Fifty or a hundred was the conventional. Still, he was sure that on various occasions he had withdrawn five hundred or even a thousand. He did not realize that his breath was rather dreadful with stale and fresh alcohol.

He hurried away from the Fifth Avenue sector where he was sure to meet someone he knew. He walked across town, back to the Pennsylvania Station, stopping at several bars for highballs. He was becoming quite tight and realized that he should be taking a train. But it was exhilarating to stick around. He wished he knew where there was a short-wave radio so he could hear the calls to the police cars.

He looked at his watch. The murder must have been discovered by this time. He wondered how long it would take them to identify the murderer. He didn't doubt that they would eventually identify him. They always did; they always got their man. But it might take quite a while.

He reasoned it out. The bell-boy would remember, that although the murderer had registered as "Peter

McCoy" the initials on the expensive bag had been "M. F." In their check of the saloons, the better saloons because the bag was a better bag, they would discover that Miles Farrington ("M. F.") had been on an all-night binge, buying liquor and cashing checks. The police wouldn't know that Miles Farrington was a man who couldn't possibly commit a murder and so they would look for corroborative facts. Probably some of the checks had his fingerprints on them. The police would compare them with the prints all over the scene of the crime and they had him. Very simple! Or, in their search for the bag, they would probably go to the railroad check rooms first of all. He wondered how long they kept unclaimed baggage. Thirty days, probably.

He wouldn't deny the crime when they caught him. But they'd have to catch him first. Suddenly, he made up his mind he wouldn't be caught. At least not alive. He'd buy a revolver in Jersey and after he had spent the five hundred dollars—

"Putting 'em away rather early today aren't you, Mr. Farrington?"

Miles did not jump or display anything more than normal surprise. He looked at the bartender who recognized him.

"You don't remember me, Mr. Farrington? I used to be at Frank's on East Fifty-fourth Street."

"Sure—sure—have a drink?"

"Thank you, sir. Celebrating something?"

"Celebrating?" Miles repeated the word. Suppose he told this bartender he was celebrating a murder. The fatuous grin would probably remain. "Yes, I'm celebrating my wife's gone to Reno!"

The fatuous grin became a little more fatuous. "Yes, sir!"

It was the first time he had thought of Brenda since he had left the hotel room. She probably would be on her way to Reno that day or the next. She wouldn't hear from him and she would take that for acquiescence. If she only knew that it wasn't necessary for her to go to Reno. She could sue in New York State, naming the murdered woman. Or she could wait until he was dead by suicide or electrocution. She probably wouldn't know that he was being sought until she arrived in Reno. She would undoubtedly fly. She always did the latest and the most expensive thing.

Miles declined a drink on the house and decided it was time to catch a train. He stopped in a liquor store, bought two pints of whiskey, and hurried on to the station. He bought all the afternoon papers in the lobby. Not a word on the first page and it would certainly have made the first page of the *Journal* if they had identified him. In fact he rather thought that after he was identified, it would be on the first page of all the papers.

He had his first sentimental thought. He was glad that his mother was dead. Then he wondered. He knew that his mother had always despised him as an ineffectual weakling. She had loathed Brenda and had cut her off without an ear-ring and had made it very pointed by leaving something to every other relative, even distant cousins. She probably would have been delighted if he had murdered Brenda.

He bought a ticket to Philadelphia. He didn't want to go too far. In Philadelphia, he would double back on his trail and return to Newark or some nearby town. Most murderers try to get too far away.

He rode in the day coach and in the men's room he destroyed all the papers and letters that he had on his person and in his wallet. He burned and threw the charred pieces through the toilet seat. In Philadelphia, he would buy an entirely new outfit, getting rid of all his clothes with tell-tale laundry and cleaners' marks.

In the smoker, a Princeton boy drank with him. "Haven't I seen you somewhere?" the boy asked.

"You might have," Miles admitted, "but it isn't very likely. I don't live in New York; this is my first visit."

"Oh—Princeton man, sir?"

"I'm not a college graduate—"

"Oh!"

"Help yourself to the bottle." Miles put it on the seat between them. "I've got to read all these papers."

He didn't read them but he examined them carefully, column by column. Not one word about the murder and not a word that he could find about a lost country girl from Pennsylvania. Of course, that might have been a lie. Well, it would be interesting to know who and what she really was. Probably one of those taxi dancers he had read about.

Between papers, he had a drink with the college boy who was still sure he'd seen Miles somewhere.

"Well what of it?" Miles demanded and then added grimly: "You see me now and I bet you'll remember it."

"Oh yes, sir, I'll remember you and may I introduce myself? I'm—"

"Please don't," Miles snapped. "Let's call it a drinking acquaintance without any obligation and let it go at that."

"But I feel there is an obligation."

Miles buried himself in another paper.

Trenton!

The boy said good bye rather sloppily. He wasn't carrying his liquor any too well.

"'Bye, sir, and I hope I have the chance to reciprocate sometime."

"You won't," Miles assured him and shook hands heartily.

Well it would be a kick for that kid when he read that he had been drinking with a murderer—a passion murderer, they would probably call him. Miles fell asleep although he realized it was a foolish thing to do.

When the train arrived at the Broad Street station, the brakeman had to shake him roughly to awaken him. But Miles betrayed no alarm or fright. He awakened groggily as any drunk would awaken.

"Have a drink," he invited the brakeman.

The brakeman declined. He was annoyed. "Get the hell out of here before I call a bull."

That aroused Miles. It wouldn't be playing the game to be arrested for drunkenness. There was one thing he must avoid—fingerprints!

He refused a taxi and suddenly realized he was very, very tired. He selected a cheap hotel in the immediate vicinity. The clerk—to dignify the tobacco-chewing custodian with that title—made him pay in advance and charged him an extortionate price but otherwise was not interested in his condition. His pen wavered over the register. Mustn't use Peter McCoy any more.

"John Smith'll do," the man said sardonically.

"My name is Mortimer Downs, junior," Miles said with great dignity, "but I don't feel like writing it."

He gave the pen to the man who laboriously wrote "Mortimer Downs, jr., City," on the register.

Pretty bright, Miles reflected; now they didn't have his handwriting to compare with that other register. The man behind the desk gave him a key and told him how to find his room. It wasn't as bad as Miles had expected. It was cleaner and brighter than the dingy entrance. Miles pulled off his coat, took another drink, and fell across the bed. He suddenly remembered the money in his pocket and aroused himself sufficiently to roll it together and put it in his sock.

He slept until daylight and awakened feeling horrible. His head was spinning and he was so weak he could hardly stand. He was alarmed. He was sure the liquor had been all right. Then he remembered that he had not eaten one mouthful the day before and nothing the night before that. He had only taken a few mouthfuls with the girl in the Eighth Avenue restaurant.

He pulled on his coat, felt the money in his sock and transferred part of it to his trousers pocket. He took a small drink; he had almost a half pint left; it strengthened him a little but he decided if he didn't get something to eat, he wouldn't be able to stand on his feet.

There was a lunch counter next to the hotel. A bum lounged in the entrance. "Buy me a cup of Java, mister?"

"Sure," Miles said. They sat at the counter together. "Order anything you want," Miles invited. He decided he'd better not have too much after a thirty-hour fast. He was about to order orange juice and then realized that this greasy place might not have such a luxury. But were oranges a luxury?

"Do you have oranges?" he asked apologetically.

"Sure," the counterman said, almost indignantly. "Sliced or juice?"

"Juice," Miles ordered. "And toast and coffee and a cooked cereal if you have it."

"Oatmeal."

Oatmeal would be fine, Miles said. The bum regretfully ordered doughnuts and coffee. He just couldn't eat anything else in the morning, he explained. Miles had no idea what time it was but apparently it was very early. Only a few trucks clattered over the streets.

They ate in silence; Miles paid the check, being careful to draw only one bill from his pocket, and then he produced his bottle. The bum accepted a drink and the counterman had one with them.

"So that's it," the bum said.

"What is it?" Miles asked. He wasn't afraid. The murder and its consequences had receded into the background of his consciousness. He had become a new human being and was enjoying it.

"The liquor," the bum explained. "I was wondering why a well-dressed gentleman would be in this part of town at this hour of the morning. Funny what liquor'll do."

"It certainly is," Miles agreed. *A well-dressed gentleman.* That was the first thing he must attend to.

"You're lucky you run into me," the bum said, "instead of some of them guys that hang around at this time of the morning."

"Why?" Miles asked. He really didn't give a damn but it was his lifelong habit to be politely social and it would take more than a murder and a few pints of liquor to change the habits of a lifetime.

"Most of them would have dragged you around the corner, knocked you over the head, and taken your roll away from you."

Now Miles was interested. "It wouldn't be so easy to drag me around the corner," he said, "and what makes you think I've got a roll on me?"

"I seen you fumbling in your pocket, picking one bill from the rest."

Miles laughed. He would have to learn some of the observing ways of the underworld if he wanted to outsmart the detectives who would be on his trail.

He stood up. "All right, Jack," he said. "You win." He gave the bum a dollar. "So long!"

"Thank you, chief. See you again sometime, maybe."
"Maybe."

He walked the streets for several hours before the cheap clothing stores opened their doors. He had several drinks of fifteen-cent whiskey. Might as well become accustomed to it. As a matter of fact, he couldn't see that it was particularly bad. Saturated as he was, it was probably difficult to tell the difference.

At first he had thought he would buy new, cheap work clothes but he decided against that. A whole outfit of new clothes was always conspicuous and he had sense enough to realize that it would take more than work clothes, especially new ones, to make him look like a laborer. So he selected a store that handled both new and second-hand clothes.

He bought a pair of new, cheap work pants. He couldn't bear the thought of second-hand trousers. Then he selected a second-hand coat and vest. He was surprised to see how easy it was to get a proper fit. He recollected how his tailor stewed and fretted and always required three or four try-ons.

"You're an actor?" the proprietor of the store suggested affably.

"What makes you think that?" Miles asked.

The man grinned. "You wouldn't he buying these clothes for any other reason. When Philadelphia was a regular show town, I used to sell second-hand clothes to actors all the time."

"I'm just an amateur," Miles said truthfully.

"Don't want to sell the clothes you have on, do you?" the man asked jocularly as he handed Miles the bundle.

Miles considered. "No, I guess not."

He went to another shop and bought a light-weight gray flannel shirt, a pair of fifteen cent socks, a ten cent tie, a twenty-five cent pair of shorts, and two five cent handkerchiefs. He decided he couldn't wear cheap, heavy work shoes as he would probably be doing a great deal of tramping around. He finally bought a pair of second-hand shoes, in good condition, for a dollar. He had all his purchases put into one large bundle.

Where to change? That was a real problem. Railroad, bus, and interurban trolley stations were probably being watched. He couldn't go into the washroom of a good hotel or bar-room as a gentleman and come out dressed as a vagrant. The same applied with more force to a cheap hotel or saloon. A Y.M.C.A.—a bath house—a church. None of them practical; some attendant would always be snooping around.

He walked into a wide boulevard that was lined with gas stations. He had an idea! All large gas stations have washrooms and toilets. Some of them are well to the side or the back and the attendants pay little or no attention to them.

The first station he selected wouldn't do. It was too elaborate and lavish in its service. The stool was in a separate compartment with a door that didn't reach to the floor. A man changing his shoes and socks would be observed by another man using the washbowl or urinal.

He found a place conducted by a less ornate corporation that wasn't burdened with a Radio City complex. Their men's room was all in one with a substantial door that locked. Miles worked fast, although he didn't think anyone had seen him go in. He examined himself, as well as he could, in the small mirror. He looked like a bum all right but it was probably more the effect of a two days' growth of beard than the clothes. He would have to shave or get shaved. He couldn't imagine anything more foolish than trying to disguise himself with a beard. If he were a detective looking for a murderer, he was sure that a bearded man would be the first to attract his attention.

He wrapped his two hundred dollar suit, his Sulka shirt, tie, and underwear, his English socks and shoes, and his Italian hat in the paper which had contained his new outfit. He had forgotten to buy a hat but that was all right. Most of the unemployed were hatless.

He got away from the gas station without attracting any attention. The attendants were busy with cars. His next problem was the bundle. The clothes in it had as many identification marks as an infected finger has germs. To throw the bundle into a trash can or even into the river would be foolhardy. It should be burned but how to burn it? Even if he wandered into the country a bonfire would attract attention.

He remembered that in cheap suburbs he had seen hideous apartment houses with signs "Electric Refrigeration and Incinerators." An incinerator was the thing. He sat down in a saloon and had a drink and a sandwich while he thought the matter out. He finally decided to ride out into one of the industrial suburbs.

He had determined not to ask questions so he spent more than an hour finding what he wanted. From the trolley he could see many low, sprawling apartment buildings which he was sure had incinerators although there was no sign to indicate it. He left the trolley and walked down the bare, treeless street.

He finally selected an apartment building that was a little more ornate than the others. The front door was open. If he met anyone, he was looking for an apartment. The entrance hall was entirely deserted. There were large jars filled with dusty artificial flowers and an unlighted electric fireplace.

There was an automatic elevator and he went to the third floor. He walked down a long hallway. If anybody asked him his business he would be looking for Mrs. Levy. In New York, he had been told it was always safe to ask for Mrs. Levy. There were as many as there were Smiths and Joneses but the name wasn't as well publicized. Maybe that wasn't true in a Philadelphia industrial suburb. Maybe Casey would be better.

His luck held. At the end of the corridor, black letters on a green steel door said INCINERATOR. He opened the door and was in a cement closet. The smell of the incinerator was unmistakable. He threw in his bundle. Then he suddenly decided to dispose of his watch, his fountain pen, his cigarette lighter, his key-case and his empty wallet in the same way. That, he realized, was probably foolish. They wouldn't burn but they would melt enough to be unrecognizable. Anyway, he felt that he couldn't face the problem of disposing of them otherwise. He suddenly felt very, very weary and sick of the whole thing. The long trolley ride had almost sobered him. The effect was terrific depression. The whole thing seemed completely futile. Of course, they would get him. It was just a question of hours or days. And the game he was playing was childish, a silly sort of realistic hounds and hares.

He tossed the accessories into the incinerator one at a time, in spite of the sign which said that tin cans, bottles and other unburnable matter were not to be put in but should be left on the floor. Well it didn't mention Tiffany watches. That watch had been the gift of his mother but Miles felt no sentiment about it. He felt no sentiment about anything and that was a great relief.

He stumbled out of the almost airless closet, walked back down the corridor, and pressed the button for the automatic elevator. It appeared almost instantly and a stout lady emerged from it. She might easily have been

Mrs. Levy. "Gut efening," she said with a friendly smile. Miles grunted and stepped into the elevator.

He was greatly relieved to be rid of all his possessions. He was sure there wasn't one thing left. But out in the air again, he still felt very sick and weary. He walked into an empty lot and vomited. That relieved him a little. Apparently, he was walking in the wrong direction. He should have reached the trolley but it was nowhere in sight.

He went into a saloon for a drink and to ask directions. He couldn't swallow the drink, however. He went into the toilet and vomited again. The bartender berated him savagely when he emerged and Miles threw him a half dollar. Anyway, he decided as he staggered out, he must look like a vagrant or the bartender wouldn't have been so savage. It would be terrible to be arrested for vomiting.

That was the one thing to be avoided; being picked up for getting into a drunken brawl or something equally trivial. Miles remembered the case of the two brothers who had been arrested as vagrants in a Long Island subway station and later convicted as long-sought gunmen and sent to the electric chair. There was no doubt that by now his fingerprints were being sent all over the country.

He remembered that he hadn't bought a New York paper. Still, he had been right in attending to his clothes and the other things that would identify him. If only he didn't feel so sick and miserable. Maybe a shave would make him feel better and build up his morale.

But the sanitary suburban barber refused to shave him and Miles realized how vile his breath and appearance must be. He went to a drug store and bought a small bottle of Listerine. He found a vacant lot and gargled and wiped his face and mouth carefully with a handkerchief. He would wait until he got back to town to get shaved. The barbers on the street where he had bought his second-hand clothing wouldn't be so fussy.

He felt terribly sick. He was sure he had a fever. Maybe it was just the effect of the liquor but he didn't think so. The street on which he was now walking was closely built up with small houses and shops. Many of the houses bore neat signs, "Furnished Rooms." He suddenly decided he would rent a room. He couldn't imagine anything more remote than this suburb and if he were going to be sick he would need a room. It wouldn't do to be taken to a hospital, public or private.

A clean-looking woman, either Scandinavian or German, was scrubbing the white stone steps of a red brick house which bore the usual sign.

"I'd like to rent a room," Miles said.

The woman looked at him critically. Apparently, the Listerine had done its work. His whiskers didn't frighten her.

"I can put you in a room with another man," she said, "for four dollars—"

"Can't I have a room by myself?" Miles interrupted.

"Yes," the woman said, wringing out her mop, "but that will cost you six dollars."

That seemed very high to Miles. Almost as high as the Ritz. Then he suddenly realized that she meant for a week.

"All right," he said, "I'd like to rent it—"

"You want to see it first, don't you?" the woman asked, getting slowly to her feet and picking up her bucket.

"I can tell from your house that it will be all right," Miles said.

She appreciated the compliment. "My house is very clean," she said, "but people won't pay for clean rooms any more; they want cheap rooms no matter how filthy they are."

The room she showed him was immaculately clean. It contained a double iron bed, a bureau, a closet, and a rocking chair. That was all. Apparently the world was full of double beds and he had never been conscious of them.

"The bathroom is right next door," the woman explained, "and whenever you want hot water, day or night, I light the heater."

Miles put his hand in his pocket. "I'll take it for a week," he said.

"I don't rent by the week, only by the month," the woman said.

Good God! Did she mean six dollars a month? But he must not betray any surprise.

"Aren't you working?" the woman asked and there was a sudden suspicion in her voice.

"That's just it," Miles explained, "my cousin thinks he can get a job for me but he isn't sure—"

"Well I'll let you have it for two dollars for one week."

"I'll pay you for two weeks," Miles said eagerly, "whether I stay or not." He handed her four dollars.

"If you don't stay," she said, "I'll give you back two dollars. When will you move in?"

Of course she would expect him to move in. "My things are in Philadelphia," he explained, "but I don't want to get them until tomorrow. I've been walking all day and I'm very tired. May I stay now?"

"Sure—sure. The bed is all made."

"Is there someplace near where I can get my dinner?"

She told him there was a little bakery down the street where he could get excellent meals. Miles thanked her and sat down on the bed. The room was spinning around.

The woman looked at him curiously. "You're sick?" she asked.

"No, I don't think so. Just tired—very tired."

"I'll make you a cup of tea—maybe?" Her sympathy was evidently aroused.

"Oh no, thank you," Miles said quickly. "I'm sure I'll be all right. I'll take a nap and then I'll go out and get some dinner."

She left the room without saying anything else. He took off his second-hand shoes and fell back on the bed. He was dozing when there was a knock on the door. He leaped up. The police couldn't have arrived that quickly. But it was only the woman bringing towels. "You have to buy your own soap," she explained, "but I'll lend you a cake until you move in tomorrow."

"I'll pay you for it," Miles said, putting his hand into his pocket. But she firmly refused to accept payment for the soap. She was lending it to him.

Miles removed his coat and tried to make himself comfortable on the bed. But he couldn't sleep although he felt terribly tired and feverish. He dozed fitfully but it wasn't really sleep. He decided hot soup and real food might be what he needed. He probably had caught cold wandering around in the rain that night. That night! It seemed so remote, so completely detached. It must have happened to another man. Certain things about it were already as dim as if it had happened years before. And only about thirty-six hours had elapsed.

He couldn't eat the food, although the bakery restaurant was everything that his landlady had said. He stopped in a drug store, for aspirin. He could barely negotiate the distance back to his room. He was sick all right and he was sure he had a high fever. It didn't matter very much, he reflected; if he got well, he was probably as safe in his rooming house as he was anywhere. If he died the thing was settled and he would be identified some way—by his fingerprints probably. He had certainly become fingerprint conscious.

He managed to get his clothes off and to hang them up. The night was fairly chilly but there were ample covers on his clean bed. He left on his shorts. The cool sheets felt fine against his feverish body. He had wild, delirious phantasies but they had nothing to do with his crime. His head floated around the room, completely detached from his body. He finally got up and turned on the light. That was better; his delirium was not so violent. Toward morning he fell into a sounder sleep. When he awakened it was broad daylight. He immediately turned out the light. He would have to give the landlady something extra for that. If she rented a room for six dollars a month, she certainly couldn't afford to have a light burning all night.

He felt a little better but he still had a fever and found that he could not stand up. He went back to bed and slept for five or ten minutes at a time. A few hours passed and there was a knock at his door. But he was not frightened. He pulled the covers up to his chin and called out: "Come in."

The landlady opened the door cautiously. "How do you feel?" she asked.

"Not very well," Miles said. "I guess I've got a bad cold or the grippe—"

"Shall I call a doctor?" the woman suggested.

"No, I won't need a doctor, I'm sure," Miles said. "I get this sort of cold almost every winter." That was true and he usually had a specialist and two nurses and recuperated in Florida or Bermuda. "Do you think you could fix me a cup of tea?"

"Sure I can and some toast too," the woman said and hurried away.

He was sure she would fix the food he needed if he paid her. But he mustn't give her too much money or she would be suspicious. He got up, and wrapping one of the blankets around him, went into the bathroom. When he returned, he took some money from his trousers and put it under his pillow. Most of his money was still in his sock.

The woman came in shortly with tea, toast, and a bottle on a tray.

"Here you are," she said briskly.

Miles thanked her and sat up. He reached under his pillow and drew out two dollars. "Here," he said, "you must take this; I know I won't be able to get out of bed today."

The woman took the bills although her manner was reluctant. "All right," she said, "I'll make you some good chicken broth for noontime and tonight a cup custard—huh?"

"That will be fine," Miles said. How lucky he was to have fallen into such good hands. The gods of chance must be having sport with him. Being fattened for the electric chair, as it were.

The woman took the bottle from the tray. "And I think what you need most is a good dose of castor oil," she said.

"You're probably right," Miles agreed.

Four

He was sick for more than a week but managed to keep a firm hold on himself. He was only delirious at night when the woman wasn't in the room and even that delirium he could control by turning on the light. The landlady was an efficient nurse without any fuss or feathers. She thought Miles' fear of doctors and hospitals was dictated by poverty and she was sympathetic with that. She had the natural distrust of the foreign-born for free wards and clinics. While she was not mercenary, she was grateful for the extra money which Miles paid her. But she proudly refused to take anything for her personal services.

Miles had the feeling that the police had undoubtedly followed his movements to Philadelphia and had lost the trail there and would not pick it up again until his unburned effects were discovered in that incinerator. He had no definite reason for thinking that but the conviction was so strong that it amounted to a certainty. His bag, the bartender who knew him, the Princeton student on the train; all or some of these things would certainly be discovered by even the dumbest detective and the hotel clerk in Philadelphia (he must remember to call it Philly) would certainly remember the man whose name he had registered. That had seemed clever at the time but now Miles realized that would only impress his identity more forcibly upon the clerk.

But he felt from then the trail was cold. They would hardly locate the second-hand stores, the lunch counter, or the gas station where he had changed clothes. So until they did locate the charred stuff in the incinerator, Miles felt he was fairly safe in his furnished room. From his bed, he could watch the passersby outside in the street. He couldn't see that any of them were particularly interested in the house. A policeman in a funny, old-fashioned uniform went by two or three times a day but never paused or looked in through the windows.

When Miles was definitely on the mend and sitting in a chair while the landlady changed the linen on the bed, she said, entirely casually with the manner of a person remembering something unimportant, that on the day he had been the sickest, two men had been inquiring for him but she wouldn't let them in. She told them they'd have to wait a few days.

His quavering voice and his shaking hands were excused by his illness. "That must have been my cousin and a friend of his," he said.

"I don't think so," the landlady replied, "they didn't seem to know your name."

"How do you know they wanted to see me then?"

The landlady explained. "They just asked me if any stranger had moved in and I said you was probably the one they was looking for but that you were too sick to have company."

Miles thought he probably should change the subject and get out as quickly as possible. He could say he was strong enough to go to the bakery for a meal. But he found it impossible to refrain from asking a few more questions.

"Did they describe me to you?" he ventured. The landlady was puzzled by the word. "I mean," he explained, "did they want to know what I looked like." He awaited the answer impatiently.

"Oh no—I don't think it was important. They probably just thought you might be an old friend."

"Yes, I guess so," Miles agreed. They couldn't have been very certain, Miles decided, or they would have shown their credentials and insisted upon seeing him. Probably the charred remains of his jewelry had been identified and they were making a half-hearted check of the entire community. They wouldn't think him foolish enough to stay in the place where he had left such easy means of identification. And he certainly would not have stayed there if he hadn't been taken ill. He'd better get out before they rechecked. Of course, if they were New York detectives it would be useless. They would probably be rooming across the street, watching his room and the house day and night.

He couldn't see anything suspicious about the row of houses across the street—no drawn curtains or darkened interiors. Particularly when they cleaned, the housewives seemed to have nothing to conceal. Miles had never realized there was such ostentatious, self-conscious cleanliness in America. It reminded him of the excesses of Holland or of some of the Swiss villages.

At that moment his landlady had tossed the mattress from his bed and was giving the spring a thorough going-over with some sort of an oiled rag. "I suppose," she said, "you'll be wanting to get word to your cousin where you are. He must be worrying about you, don't you think?"

"Oh no, he won't be worrying," Miles explained; "he's accustomed to my comings and goings. And I don't know just where he lives—I'll have to see him at the place where he works."

The landlady asked no further questions. Very fortunately, she seemed to have very little curiosity. Miles had always thought that landladies were abnormally inquisitive but this one took no more than a polite interest in his affairs. However, Miles didn't allow himself to be too reassured by that. Apparently, she didn't keep in touch with the world in general. She did not own a radio and did not take a daily paper. So far as

Miles could see, there wasn't even a foreign language newspaper around the place.

When he made his first trip to the bakery-restaurant he picked up a Philadelphia paper (they only had the current issue) but he could not find any reference to himself or the murder for which he was wanted. But it seemed to him that the New York news was meagre. When he was reasonably sure that he wasn't being followed (and it seemed rather careless of the two men who had been asking for him) he went to other stands and bought all the Philadelphia papers, one at each place, but the search was fruitless. If the murder of the obscure little girl in the Broadway hotel had been news in Philadelphia, its pull had not been sufficient to last a week.

When he stepped into the hallway on his return, the landlady met him. "Those two fellows are in the parlor," she said, pointing with her thumb. Miles wondered why they hadn't taken him in the street. How could they have been so sure he would return to his room? And what a fool he had been to return.

It would be silly to run for it now. They would take a shot at him through the window. He had determined that he wouldn't be taken alive but he felt a certain curiosity about these men. Apparently, they weren't certain of him or they would have pounced down on him long ago. It would be fun if he could bluff them. He could always make a break for it and have them shoot him. He walked into the parlor.

The men, he decided at a glance, were detectives. Their huge flat feet, their red faces, and their absurd attempt at disguise; their shirts, carelessly open at the throat and without ties, were much too clean and new. Even he had done better than that in his impersonation of a worker.

"Feeling better?" one of them asked. "You was pretty sick when we dropped in the other day."

Miles noted the carefully incorrect you was.

"I'm feeling some better," he answered, "but pretty weak."

"You don't look so chipper," the man agreed. "You're a stranger around here, aren't you?"

"Yes, I am," Miles admitted and then decided to force the issue. "Who are you fellows anyway and what the hell do you want with me?"

They didn't seem to resent the question. "We're just a couple of boys from the Snelling plant," the spokesman said; "you see we've got a strike call out for Monday and we hear the company is bringing in strike-breakers."

Miles laughed at first quietly and then hysterically. He quickly checked that but he couldn't avoid the outburst. The men looked at him with a little alarm as if they feared his illness might have been mental.

"I'm not a strike-breaker," he assured them hastily. "I have a cousin here who thought he might get me a job but it wouldn't be strike-breaking."

"Well, if you're looking for a job," his questioner said belligerently, "where's your union card?"

"Well, you see," Miles explained apologetically, "I— I'm not exactly a working-man—it was sort of a white-collar job I was looking for."

The second man joined the conversation for the first time. "You don't look as if you'd ever done much work," he said contemptuously; "maybe you're representing one of them Fink companies that are going to bring in scabs."

Miles assured them earnestly and a trifle firmly, now that he was sure they were not detectives, that he was not representing anybody but was looking for a decent, honest job that wouldn't interfere with anybody else. He wished he said *nobody else* but he hadn't thought of it in time.

They studied him carefully. "The Finks wouldn't be sending out a guy like him," the first man said. "Well you soft guys are learning what it is to be up against it—don't you think it's time you was getting wise to yourselves and joining up?"

"Maybe you're right," Miles admitted. "I don't know much about it. I've always been in business for myself."

"You haven't been very well," the second man said, "and it ain't going to do your health no good to stay in this town. We don't like guys here without union cards, no matter what kind of job you're looking for."

"What's your cousin's name?" the first man asked.

"George Fowler," Miles said. He had decided on that name to give the landlady but she had not asked for it.

Neither of the union delegates had ever heard of George Fowler.

"He may have left here," Miles said. "He's a great fellow to wander around."

"No use roaming around the country looking for work," the first man said, getting up from his chair. "If you can't get work at home you might as well go on relief and be done with it."

Miles was so confident now that he couldn't refrain from giving a little lecture. "That's the trouble," he said, "too many people are going on relief rolls without making any real effort to go to work."

"Oh, yeah?" the second man said. "Well it's better to go on relief than to pull down the wages of those who have work; and you don't see any of the rich guys refusing anything from the government do you? Only they ask for it in thousands not in two-bit pieces."

Miles thought it better not to claim any acquaintance with, or knowledge of, the rich. The first man moved over to the door.

"C'mon, Joe," he said. "I guess this buddy is all right—he just ain't been around much."

They went out and the landlady immediately hurried into the room. She was indignant. "Them big bums!" she said. "Going around telling people they can't work! I think they're making good wages when you think about the price of canned goods in the market." It was a cannery they worked for, she explained.

Miles sighed. He felt that for the time being he had trouble enough of his own without tackling the labor question.

"I might have argued with them," he said, "but I'm not strong enough to go to work. I guess I'd better go home for a while."

The landlady was sympathetic but, like his two inquisitors, she apparently realized that he was not a working man. However, she was not suspicious. Miles looked even less like a murderer than he did a working man. She hated to lose him, and she hoped he'd be all right, and she absolutely refused the extra five dollars which he tried to press on her. In fact, she wanted to return part of his rent. Miles decided that landladies were greatly maligned.

He felt completely relaxed and gorgeously free after the false alarm. But he knew he ought to move on. If his charred jewelry had not yet been discovered in the incinerator ashes, it was only a question of time until it would be found and identified. Philadelphia wasn't safe, of course. He probably ought to double back and go to Newark or maybe Boston but he felt too indolent and listless to travel and he sort of liked it around Philadelphia. It was clean and friendly. If he were in

Newark, he was sure he'd be unable to resist the temptation to go into New York sometime and in Boston he knew a great many people.

He decided he would stop over in downtown Philadelphia just long enough to get the New York newspapers. But just as he was about to step up to the newsstand he had another thought. If they were looking for a man from New York where would be the most natural place to pick him up? At a newsstand buying a New York paper, of course! It wasn't likely that all the places selling New York papers in Philadelphia could be covered but probably all of them had been furnished with his description and if there were a reward offered, the paper venders would be keeping a sharp lookout and, with the exception of his clothes, he had done nothing to change his appearance. He felt sure there must be a reward offered for his capture, dead or alive. Either the hotel, or the hotel men's association or some organization or another must have offered a reward. After all, hotels must have some way of protecting themselves against promiscuous murderers.

Feeling that he had again cleverly avoided a pitfall, Miles veered away from the newsstand and into a saloon. It seemed to him that he had been eyed very sharply by the news-vender. After all, why should he want to see the newspapers? It was just morbid curiosity. Perhaps it would be better for his peace of mind if he didn't see the stuff that had been printed. He wondered if they had obtained or stolen a photograph of him. He hadn't any idea what had become of his mother's collection. He hadn't had any taken since her death.

A drink was just what he needed. He hadn't realized how weak he was. He had two more immediately and felt much better. He would have liked to have seen the papers and to have learned what his partners had said.

He was sorry for them; they were good fellows and, in their way, fond of him, especially George Sherman. For years they had tactfully and persistently tried to get him to leave Brenda. Now, they would undoubtedly claim that he had been out of his mind. Probably they would hire the best possible criminal lawyers to prove it.

Had he been? Had it been temporary insanity or just plain ordinary intoxication. Miles couldn't make up his mind. He'd have to leave it to the experts and the jury, he supposed. He had been drunk before but he had never harmed anyone. Of course, he hadn't meant to kill her. Or had he? He couldn't be sure. He suddenly realized that after he had two or three drinks he only thought about the crime itself; when he was sober his thoughts were exclusively of escape and avoiding the police. His drunken thoughts were much more exhilarating; he would stay drunk.

He had no future to think about except the electric chair or the insane asylum. All his life he had worried about his future. His lack of brilliance as a student had been a great trial to his mother who belonged to a family of mental prodigies. Of course she blamed it all on his paternal side. By terrific work, Miles had made Phi Beta Kappa but it was the triumph of a grind, not an intellectual. And then he had worried about a career, not realizing that the family money would take care of that. As it happened, his collegiate friendship with George Sherman and his gift for hard work were chiefly responsible for his business success. Then he had worried about getting Brenda to marry him; after she had married him, he worried more about keeping her married to him.

Well, it had all ended in murder and he had nothing to worry about except capture and the electric chair, the one thing in life he had never contemplated or considered. He remembered a boyhood playmate who was always in mortal terror of being electrocuted for a crime he had not committed. Miles had thought that silly. A Farrington couldn't possibly be accused of murder. He had never been able to make up his mind whether he believed in capital punishment. It had always been so completely theoretical. As he took another drink, he realized this was a great simplification. All the troubles, worries and annoyances of life had been concentrated into one major plight.

He wandered aimlessly from cheap saloon to cheap saloon, eventually reaching the waterfront. Across the river—he supposed it was a river—he could see church steeples and the smoke stacks of many factories and industrial plants.

"Is that another part of Philly?" he asked the bartender and congratulated himself upon having achieved *Philly* at last.

The bartender laughed heartily. "Those are fighting words, brother," he said. "You must be a greenhorn. That's Camden, New Jersey."

New Jersey! Then the Philadelphia police who were on the lookout for him wouldn't be able to get him and in Jersey the trail was probably cold by this time.

"What's the best way to get there?" he asked.

"Well, the best way," the bartender said carefully, "is a bus over the bridge but the cheapest way is by ferry—that only costs a couple of coppers."

Miles decided to go by ferry; not for reasons of economy because the necessity of holding on to his money hadn't as yet become vital. However, the ferry trip appealed to him. It seemed a less conspicuous way of traveling than by bus.

He drank his way from the ferry-slip up into the heart of Camden. He realized as he progressed that

Camden divided its allegiance between the Victor talking machine and the memory of Walt Whitman. All other industries were secondary.

He found the whiskey of Jersey a little cheaper and just as potent as that of Philadelphia. He had started drinking cheap whiskey as part of the vague character he was impersonating, and after a few drinks he couldn't see much difference between it and the bonded brands and the fine Scotch to which he was accustomed. Of course he knew there was a great difference but apparently he did not have the necessary refinement of taste to appreciate the difference. He seemed to get drunk quicker on the cheaper brands and, after all, that was the only object.

He spent the night in a cheap, dirty hotel and paid a dollar and a half for the privilege. The next morning he went room hunting. They were more expensive and not so clean as the one in the Pennsylvania suburb but he finally found a satisfactory cubby-hole for three dollars a week.

"I suppose you're trying to get on with the Victor people?" the landlady said as he paid her a week's rent in advance.

"I've been promised a job," Miles said cautiously, "but I've been sick and I'm going to rest for a week first."

"There's plenty of people resting these days," the woman philosophized. "I've only got one rule here, mister. No women in the room."

"All right," Miles agreed. When had someone called him "mister" before? He remembered.

Apparently his offhand agreement didn't carry conviction. "I mean it," the woman said emphatically. "God knows I expect people to be human but when you have a lot of men roomers you can't let them bring women in. Sooner or later there's a big row and the police get down on you."

"All right," Miles repeated, "I won't bring any women in."

"Of course I don't mind if you want to bring a friend in occasionally in the afternoon while you're not working. I want you to feel at home but no company after dark. An' no loud talking day or night."

It was like boarding school. "Don't you think," Miles suggested, "that you might wait and see what I do?"

The woman did not realize she was being rebuked. "I like to have everything understood," she said firmly. "If I wasn't particular, I'd never have to have a room empty. You look quiet and respectable enough but I've noticed it's the quiet ones who are the most ornery when they get drunk."

Later that day, Miles bought a cheap straw suitcase, another shirt, a change of underwear and socks, and moved into his new home. Then he took up the routine of his life—drinking most of the night (he soon found the dives where he could drink after legal closing hours) and sleeping nearly all day. He spent practically nothing for food.

He formed a friendship with a young fellow who roomed in the same house—a drinking friendship. Joe worked in the shipyards and told Miles to stick around; he'd probably be able to land a job. The shipyards were expecting a big government contract and that would mean the employment of more men. But, Joe said gravely, Miles would have to ease up on the drinking. The company had spotters all over town. Joe, himself, only got sloppy drunk on Saturday nights; other nights he was just drunk and always went home when the legal saloons closed down or even a little earlier. But Miles was sloppy drunk every night. But Miles felt no interest in the shipbuilding plans of his country and continued to get sloppy drunk every night.

He wasn't drinking because his conscience troubled him. The death of the little street-walker seemed to have no more importance than the swatting of a fly. He was drinking as a gesture of independence and to celebrate his release from a lifetime of responsibilities, obligations and worries. Not to give a damn . . . not to give a goddamn; it was the most exhilarating sensation in the world to a man who had devoted his lifetime fulfilling the obligations of a son, a husband, and a friend. Now, as he saw it, his only obligation was to the state; the forfeiture of his life, and he wasn't going to worry about that obligation. He was going to evade it as long as possible.

On careful consideration, both drunk and sober, he decided that the thing he enjoyed most was the freedom from shaving. He had always hated to shave. As a young man he had gone to barber shops but as he grew older he discovered barbers shaved him too closely and that his neck was always sore. He had to learn to shave himself but it never ceased to be a tiresome occupation. He had a heavy beard and when he had an evening engagement, which during the winter season was practically every night, he had to shave twice a day. Now, in his exile, he shaved about every third day and he only removed the top layer. A real beard, he decided, would immediately attract the attention of a keen-eyed detective but a stubble merely gave him the effect of a bum and yet acted as a very effective disguise.

Another change in the habits of a lifetime was not so enjoyable. He soon discovered that daily bathing aroused antagonism and suspicion in the rooming house. Joe, his friend, decided he must have vermin. "You'll never get rid of 'em by washing," he advised. "They thrive on water. Get you some larkspur." And the landlady said she couldn't be supplying a tankful of hot water to him every morning. Also, he found two towels a week somewhat inadequate and bought a few from the ten-cent store. These, he carefully concealed in his straw suitcase as if they constituted a secret vice of some sort.

Joe said if Miles had a couple of extra dollars for entertainment he knew where they could get a couple of skirts. Joe had no extra money. Everything except his subsistence was seized by court order for alimony and support of his children. His money for liquor was obtained by cutting down on food and also by cheating on overtime pay, which the court (and his wife) hadn't discovered.

Miles agreed that the suggestion was a good one. Not that he felt any necessity for women, socially or physically. His years of fidelity to Brenda had stifled his natural impulses and his natural impulses were probably on the sub-sensual side. However, he was anxious to test and indulge his new freedom.

The trysting place was a saloon and Miles, finding the ladies rather dull conversationally, suggested an immediate adjournment to bed. The girls were indignant.

"What do you think we are," the more articulate one of the two demanded, "a coupla tarts?"

"Yes, aren't you?" Miles insolently responded.

The lady retorted with a glass of beer thrown in Miles' face and it was a nice, clean face, especially shaven for the occasion. The waiter hurried over. "Hey, cut that out," he said to the assaulting lady. "Where do you think you are—at home?" They were all so sensitive.

The lady pushed back her chair. "C'mon, Hilda," she said to her companion, "we ought to've knowed better." She turned to Joe. "You son-of-a-bitch!"

Hilda, looking a bit regretful, meekly followed her indignant companion out of the place.

"Jees' Christ, what'd you go and do that for?" Joe complained to the astonished and bewildered Miles. "You didn't have to rush things so."

"I was only going by what you said," Miles explained. "If I made a mistake, I'm awfully sorry—"

"Oh, they'd of taken the brute all right but they don't like to be rushed," Joe explained. "They like to have enough liquor under the skin so's they can pretend to be drunk. They don't want people to think they're regular whores."

"Don't they want money? You mean they're afraid of losing their amateur standing?"

"They'd probably ask for breakfast money and cab fare in the morning but they're the kind that pretend they do it 'cause they get plastered and like a guy," Joe explained knowingly.

"Well, that's too bad," Miles apologized; "you should have told me."

"Forget it," Joe said. "There's more'n one knothole in a fence, ain't there?"

A few nights later they were solicited to buy drinks for a couple of girls who were more friendly and, also, more commercial. Perversely, Miles was annoyed. He enjoyed drinking with these girls and didn't want to be rushed into a business transaction. One of them had selected him and assigned her companion to Joe.

"You look like Wheeler and Woolsey," she said to Miles.

"Which one?" he asked. "I can't look like both of them. You mean I look like one and Joe the other."

She laughed heartily at that. "No, no," she said, and then in a whisper, "your boy friend looks like a bird dog. No, you look like Wheeler and Woolsey. I don't know which one. I don't know them apart but you look like them."

Miles invited her to have another drink. But she was coy. She couldn't sit around wasting her time. If there were five dollars for the night in it, all right; otherwise, she'd have to be on to richer fields. Joe heard that and motioned to Miles to follow him to the toilet. There, while he relieved his bladder, he offered counsel.

"Don't let that gold-digger get into you," he said. "Two bucks if you have to rent a room; three if she's got one. Don't let her play you for a sucker."

"I won't," Miles promised. Somehow Joe's advice sounded very reminiscent. He had been hearing it in one form or another since prep school days.

They joined the ladies. Miles' companion was contemptuous.

"What's the matter?" she asked. "Do you have to ask your boy friend if you can play games or was you wiping his behind for him?"

"Joe's okay," Miles said, trying desperately to slip into the vernacular. "He's a good guy."

The girl was skeptical. "Is he? Well, do I get it?"

"Get what?"

"Say, don't play dumb. You know what—five bucks, Roosevelt money."

Miles was annoyed. He gulped down the raw whiskey which the waiter had just brought. "Quit pestering me," he said sharply. "The last woman who pestered me got killed."

His companion found that amusing. She laughed and then suddenly leaned over and kissed him sloppily. "You ain't so tough," she said.

That sloppy, greasy kiss turned his stomach. He pushed back his chair and threw a dollar on the table.

"That's for the time you've wasted," he said harshly. "I don't want any part of you."

Joe hurried after him. His only complaint was about the dollar Miles had squandered.

"You don't seem to understand dames," he said.

"No, I guess I don't," Miles admitted. "Anyway, I'm not feeling good. I'm going home."

Joe understood. "Okay, pal," he said and turned away.

Miles didn't go home. He went to a saloon in another part of town and became sloppily drunk in a very short time. He was furious with himself for having made that remark about killing a woman. If he were going to start talking that way, he might as well give himself up to the police and have done with it. What was he doing fooling around with women and friends anyway? He didn't feel the slightest need for companionship. All he wanted to do was to drink and to be perfectly free. Now, he understood hermits. A man wasn't free, if there really was such a thing as freedom, as long as he had one companion.

The next night he told Joe he was going to move. He didn't want Joe to think he was running away. That might make Joe suspicious.

"I can't afford three dollars a week for a room until I get a job," he explained. "I have to get something for about ten a month."

Joe suggested they double up but that was the last thing in the world Miles wanted to do. However, he didn't like to hurt Joe's feelings.

"No," he explained, "I can't room with anybody. Some nights I don't sleep at all and am awfully restless."

Joe agreed that wouldn't do. He had to have his sleep or he couldn't be at work at seven-thirty in the morning. So they parted, Joe urging Miles to keep in touch with him so he could get him a job when the yards got the new contracts.

But Miles didn't keep in touch with Joe. He was afraid of companionship. He had no illusions about Joe or anybody else, desperate for money. Who wouldn't go after a reward! By this time Miles had convinced himself there was a price on his head. He wasn't bitter merely because he believed money was stronger than friendship. Money was beginning to have a new value to him now that he realized his independence and freedom would be gone when his money was exhausted. And Miles remembered how his friends had sold out one another in 1929 and later; how pools and contracts had been broken and promises forgotten.

He found a room for ten dollars a month in a house that didn't have any hot water. But by that time he had learned about the municipal baths and patronized them. He was conserving his money and worrying about the inevitable time when it would be gone. He might just as well have drawn a thousand or two thousand when he left New York; he had money on deposit in three or four banks although he generally used only the one that was most convenient. But when he had fled from New York he had not dreamed that he would be at liberty for more than three or four days and five hundred dollars seemed ample. Suddenly, he remembered he had a small fortune in actual cash in a safe deposit box. He had placed it there on Brenda's advice after the bank holiday. Brenda at that time had a morbid fear of being without cash.

It gave him a great satisfaction to realize how she must be stewing now. And that was another thing to remember. The police might relax in their efforts to get him but Brenda never would. She needed him for money. In spite of her lover's monogrammed clothes and extravagant display, Miles knew that Lester Nobel had very little money. Miles wondered if his partners would give Brenda an allowance. He doubted it. They all hated her. They would all blame her for Miles' downfall. Well, it was her fault, although it was doubtful if a jury could be made to see it.

When his money was gone, he realized that he would be definitely up against it. Getting a job, conceding that one might be available, would mean giving a personal history. He couldn't apply for state relief; he couldn't prove legal residence. And he heard that the police kept a strict checkup on the transient camps which the Federal government provided for floaters.

So he became more and more miserly. He drank only in the cheapest saloons and no longer patronized after-hour resorts. Instead he provided himself, during the first weeks, with a half pint and, later, with a pint of the cheapest rot-gut he could find. He would have given up drinking in saloons altogether, except that he lived on free lunch and handouts from bartenders.

To his amazement, bartenders seemed to like him and were always giving him a cup of coffee or a sandwich. He was a quiet, harmless stew and he always had a dime for his whiskey. Some of them called him the professor because of his ability to answer questions—the constant questions which come up in any bar-room, conversation: Where was Napoleon born? On what ship did Kitchener go down? Who was heavyweight champion before Dempsey? What relation were Teddy and Franklin D. and Franklin D.'s wife? When did prohibition go into effect? What was the difference between stout and porter in the process of manufacture?

For almost the first time, Miles found his encyclopedic mind an asset; whenever he answered a question, and thereby settled an argument, someone would buy him a drink. It made him more conversational. He tried to think up subjects, tactfully, of course, which would start an argument. When the weather became very cold somebody gave him a well-worn overcoat. That coat meant more to Miles than any article of clothing he had ever owned.

In his few sober, introspective moments, he wondered how a man could sink so quickly. According to the rules of literature, motion pictures, and welfare statistics, Miles felt sure it should have been a much more gradual process. There had been no way stations. He had gone from the top of a Park Avenue apartment to the gutter almost as quickly as if he had leaped on that momentous night.

But deep within him, Miles knew that he hadn't really sunk to the gutter. Put him back into the old apartment without the shadow of the electric chair and the stigma of Brenda's desertion and he would be just the same as always. He had not really become an alcoholic. He was acting a part and having a grand time doing it. Each day he sought a new degradation, a new device to widen the breach between Miles Farrington and Mike, the bum, the professor. Mike was the name he gave to bartenders, and bartenders and barflys were the only people with whom he now had social intercourse.

He bought two dark flannel shirts and no other clothing after his first purchases. These shirts he wore a week at a time; later on, two weeks at a time. He wore no underwear. He had the shirts washed in a Chinese laundry—his one extravagance. In spite of the fact that he often slept where he fell—in dark hallways, or vacant lots, he was never robbed. No one could imagine that this filthy bum had money concealed in both filthy socks. And even when he was very drunk, he was still a fairly light sleeper. The fear of arrest always hung over him.

He became known to the police and they would almost gently kick him awake and send him home. They knew he had a room and wondered how he paid for it. He always tried to go home because he knew if the police once took him in and booked him, he was caught. That, he realized, had now become his greatest danger—being picked up for something trivial and completely unimportant in itself. So instead of avoiding the police he made a point of sticking around the neighborhood where they knew him and regarded him as a harmless stew. They, too, occasionally staked him to a cup of coffee and that afforded him a great deal of amusement.

One night a man came into the saloon where Miles was drinking and said he needed some men to load some trucks. There'd be good money in it as it was an emergency, rush job. Miles, who had just awakened from a long, refreshing sleep and had only taken several drinks, volunteered. He was worrying more and more about his vanishing money and this would give him a chance to pick up a few dollars. It was emergency employment and no questions would be asked.

He worked until four in the morning and received five dollars in pay. That was more than he had expected. He thought it would be about fifty cents an hour. Five dollars was a lot of money. It represented fifty drinks—five more days of freedom and liberty. Ten drinks a night had become his ration, except occasionally when he went on a real spree.

Then suddenly he realized that he felt terrible. Every bone and muscle in his body ached. It was more physical labor than he had ever done in his life. The saloons were closed and he would have to find one of the after-hour joints. The cheapest one he knew was down by the waterfront. But he took a wrong turn and discovered that he was lost in a maze of railroad tracks, docks and sheds.

He felt horribly, terribly sick. Worse than he had that day when he had rented a room in the Philadelphia suburb. He had not eaten for more than twenty-four hours and his system, accustomed to at least a pint of alcohol a day, was revolting. But Miles didn't think of that. He just thought he must be dying. He must find some sheltered spot and lie down. If he fell, wandering about, he'd freeze to death before morning. It was a bitter cold night. Of course, if he were dying, it didn't matter much. In fact he had heard that freezing was painless and rather pleasant. Still, he pushed on.

He felt a heavy hand on his shoulder. A watchman, not a city policeman, had caught him.

"Stealing coal, huh?" the watchman accused.

"What the hell would I want with coal?" Miles snarled. It was a bad approach. He tried to break away but the grip of the guard was firm.

He spun Miles around. "Let's have a look at you," he said.

Something in the guard's voice frightened Miles as he had not been frightened in weeks. He managed to jerk himself free from the heavy hand and started to run. They'd never take him alive. He had sworn to that. He heard several shots but he did not think he had been hit. He did not know that the guard was merely amusing himself and frightening his victim by firing into the air.

Miles leaped from the dock into the icy water. Then the guard was annoyed. He blew sharply on the police whistle which he carried in his pocket and leaped in after the derelict.

Five

Again Miles awakened to consciousness, as on that morning in the hotel room, completely at a loss as to his surroundings and the course of events that had brought him there. But this time his memory did not completely return. There was a gap. He remembered diving from the dock into the icy water and hitting something—possibly the side of a barge. Beyond that—nothing.

He recognized a strong medicinal odor even before he opened his eyes. Then he looked around. Undoubtedly, he was in a hospital. He was surrounded by beds, most of them occupied. But was he under arrest? There were no policemen in sight and surely if it were a prison hospital there would be bars at the windows; the windows were unencumbered and opened. Through the doorway, he could see a nun moving about in the hall. There was a crucifix at the foot of his bed. Undoubtedly, he was in a Catholic hospital.

A nurse looked down at him. She did not smile but her voice was pleasant enough as she said: "So you've come around, have you?"

"What's the matter with me?" Miles asked. He noticed that it hurt to talk and that his voice was weak and unnatural in sound.

The nurse picked up the chart attached to the foot of the white iron bed. "Exposure; alcoholism, acute; congestion of the lungs; under-nourishment," she read in a business-like tone. "We thought you were due for pneumonia," she said, "but you missed it and you look better now." She stuck a thermometer into his mouth and walked on to the next bed.

Miles lay back on his pillow. He felt tired; very, very tired. The nurse returned and looked at the thermometer. "You've still got a little fever. Take it easy."

She started to move away again. Miles called her back.

"Am I under arrest?" he asked.

"No," she said, looking at him for the first time with a little more personal interest; "this isn't the police ward. What would they be arresting you for?"

Irish, obviously. Miles just grinned and drifted away again. He was feverish for several more days and then when the fever was gone he felt very weak. He was content to lie there with his eyes closed and take the liquid nourishment they brought him. But it was good to be clean again and the coarse hospital gown was pleasant even if it did smell horribly of disinfectants.

They told him since he had no fever, he must try to get up and go to the toilet. But his knees crumpled and he fell to the floor when he attempted it. After that they let him rest again for several days. Then he was able to sit up and wash himself and eat a little cereal and toast. The next time he tried to stand on his feet, he didn't faint but the orderly had to help him back from the toilet. It was a slow business. He hadn't realized he was in such shocking physical condition. But when he remembered how he had worked, without having eaten in twenty-four hours, to say nothing of the immersion into the icy water, it was remarkable that he was alive at all.

Suddenly he realized that even the thought of a drink nauseated him. That phase of his flight from reality had passed. He supposed he was absolutely penniless. He wasn't sure how much he had in his socks when he dived from the dock, but it was more than a hundred and fifty dollars. Probably, the guard or the police had confiscated it.

Then the first day they gave him a real meal, a nun came to question him. His first impulse was to tell them that his name was Miles Farrington and that he was wanted in New York for murder. But the impulse passed before the words were out. Let them catch him. Since he wasn't in the police ward, he doubted if they had taken his fingerprints.

The nun who interrogated him wrote his answers down on a form. She wrote in a strangely mechanical manner and, in fact, there was something very robotlike about her. Some of the nuns he had noticed were very young and pretty but this one was not young and she was not pretty. Nor was she old and homely. She was just expressionless and ageless. A recording angel, as she sat writing; a recording angel of a mechanical age. He thought that perhaps she was a product of the Victor plant.

His name was Michael Fowler, he said; the last place where he worked was Boston (he knew Boston if they tried to check him on that) but he had not been there for more than three years. He had just been wandering around looking for work. The last people he worked for, excepting the night when he jumped into the water, had gone out of business. He hadn't really intended to commit suicide. He had just thought he was being arrested—the guard had accused him of stealing coal—and he had run for it and fallen into the water. He must have been sick then. He explained to the sister that he had been working hard and hadn't eaten for twenty-four hours. She wrote down his answers without any comment.

He had no relatives, he went on in response to her queries, no friends, nobody with whom he wanted to communicate. Then, finally, when she had gone through the printed form, she looked up at him.

"You aren't a regular vagrant, Michael Fowler," she said in a clipped, mechanical voice.

"How do you know, Sister?" he asked and he noticed that he was using the voice of Miles Farrington and not the grumbled, harsh snarls of Mike the barfly.

"I can tell," the nun replied. "I've been in this ward for many years."

"There are many vagrants now," Miles pointed out, "who haven't been vagrants before."

The nun sighed. "That is very true," she admitted, "but I'm sure you must have some friends. Won't you let me write to them?"

"No," he said firmly, "let it go, Sister, the way I've given it to you."

"All right," she agreed. She stood up and then looked at the statistical sheet on which she had been writing. "You have $162.40 in the vault, you know. It was brought in with you."

Miles was astonished. "Honest policemen here in Camden," he said.

She smiled cynically and he felt that his case was exceptional. "You'll be charged a dollar a day for the time you've been here," the nun explained.

"That's fair enough," Miles agreed; "how much longer will they keep me?"

"A week anyhow. It will take that long for you to get your strength back. You're fortunate that you are here; in Philadelphia the charity wards are so crowded, they have to turn the patients out before they are properly well."

"I'll remember that," Miles said, "and always starve and jump off the dock in Camden."

She did not return the smile. She shook her head reprovingly.

"It's a wicked thing to take the life which the Blessed Lord has given you."

Miles recognized the propaganda touch. What would she say if she knew he had taken another life? Probably, she wouldn't be surprised; if she had been in that charity ward for years, she had probably heard and seen many things.

"I didn't try to commit suicide," Miles insisted. Apparently he could not lie to this inscrutable nun. "I was just trying to get away from the officer. I didn't know what I was doing."

Another opening. "Won't you let us help you find some spiritual strength as well as physical?" she asked. Miles felt that the question was as routine as those on the printed slip which she had filled in. Perhaps it was on the printed slip.

"I think I've found it," Miles said gently; "I don't think I'll ever touch another drop of liquor as long as I live."

"That is good," she said, "but there are many abstainers who will not be given the key to Heaven." She picked up her papers. "You're not a Catholic?"

"Not a Roman Catholic," Miles answered.

Now she was sure he was not an ordinary vagrant and she walked away. She recognized the retort of an educated Episcopalian.

In a few days they took him to the roof where convalescents were given air and sun. There were many patients there, men and women, some in wheel chairs, some on crutches and a few allowed to walk freely about. A nurse and an orderly were always on duty but otherwise there wasn't anything in particular to suggest an institution. It was a relief from the ward which reeked of disinfectants and bed-pans.

The patients were friendly. They were derelicts, perhaps, but entirely different from the barflys who had been Miles' only associates during the past weeks. These people eagerly read the daily papers and the magazines which were provided for them. They were well-informed and discussed things on about the same level of enlightenment and stupidity as his former associates on Park Avenue.

One woman did not join in the discussions. She lay wrapped in her wheel chair and seemed completely inanimate. Miles wondered if she could be paralyzed. Then one day his chair was next to hers and he was surprised to see that she was quite young and pretty. And certainly not paralyzed. She didn't look very sick and the expression in her eyes was one of defiance rather than defeat. Miles was interested but she did not respond to his advances.

"Are you getting well?" he asked.

She looked at him very steadily and gave no indication that she understood the question. He wondered if she were foreign; French perhaps. Then she turned away. "I don't want to get well," she said in perfectly good nasal English. That was all and Miles couldn't think of a suitable reply, particularly as she had turned away from him. She kept turned away from him the rest of the afternoon and, of course, Miles made no further attempt to talk to her.

He questioned the orderly discreetly. "Just another one of them things," the orderly said with a wink. "I don't know why they bother to keep 'em alive."

Miles had no idea what *one of them things* meant but he supposed the orderly was reflecting on the young lady's morals. He asked no further questions but somehow she fascinated him. He felt that her despair was somehow akin to his, although he had no idea why he thought that. He was always watching her particularly when she wasn't facing in his direction. If she was conscious of his vigilance she gave no indication, except to turn away whenever their eyes met.

One afternoon when the nurse and the orderly were busy, the girl leaped from her wheel chair and was almost over the parapet when Miles caught her. She had moved with lightning speed and he reached her by a split second. It took all his strength, and he had very little, to hold her.

She screamed at him. "God-damn you! Let me go."

But he was determined to save her life. Later, he thought it might have been a subconscious desire to make up for the life he had taken. But that was a thought in retrospect. At the time, his action had been entirely instinctive and the natural result of his interest in her. She lay on the roof, sobbing and cursing. Miles held her and after a few seconds she didn't fight any more.

"You'll want to live tomorrow," Miles said, feeling the remark was very big-brotherly and inadequate. "I jumped off a dock a few weeks ago and I know what I'm talking about."

"I wish to Christ you'd drowned!" she said.

"I'm glad I didn't," he said emphatically.

She put her finger to her nose and turned away from him. The nurse came running over and took charge. All the patients were taken down to their wards and Miles heard that the orderly was discharged.

The girl was not allowed on the roof again but Miles was permitted to visit her in the women's ward. In twenty-four hours her mood had changed just as Miles had sagely predicted it would.

"I suppose I ought to thank you," she said apologetically, "but *I* don't know—"

"I don't want any thanks," Miles said cheerfully, "but you will be glad. Suicide is silly. Particularly when you're so young. You can't always have bad luck."

He felt he was being offensive but he wanted to talk to this girl and didn't have the faintest idea what to say, so he took refuge in cliches and maxims. But the girl seemed to accept them in a new, friendly spirit.

"I guess you're right," she said, "but Fate or whatever you call it has certainly been handing it out to me. I guess I've been a bum sport," she admitted. "It's been my own fault."

Suddenly, he realized that she was telling him her story. At first he was embarrassed. It was a story for a priest, not a casual visitor. But, apparently, she felt that since he had saved her life, he ought to know all about it.

There had been an illegal operation (so that was what the orderly meant) and she had almost died. They had brought her to the hospital and the man who had been responsible had not appeared or sent any word or any money. Miles pointed out that, undoubtedly, the man was afraid of arrest and in hiding. He was facing a very serious charge; murder, if she had died.

But the girl couldn't accept that theory. "He could fix anything," she explained, "and there were plenty of others he could have sent."

She had heard, she went on, that he was in Atlantic City, promoting a cabaret for his newest girl friend. He was a promoter now; he had risen from the ranks— ordinary stick-up, bootlegger, racketeer and now a bigshot promoter.

"I shouldn't think he would have deserted you completely," Miles said. "You know so much about him."

"That'd be a sure way of committing suicide," the girl said. "I don't believe I could touch him no matter what I'd say, and what proof have I? Even the doctor didn't see him. But I couldn't do nothin' to him even if I wanted to take the chance of being rubbed out. That's the kind of a poor sap I am. I still love the bastard."

"You'll get over that," Miles assured her. "I loved a woman like that for more than twelve years and I got over it in one night."

It was true. From the moment he realized that he had killed the little bum of the streets, he had been entirely indifferent to Brenda. And the only time he thought of her he enjoyed picturing her frustration at not being able to locate him.

The girl was interested. "You know all the answers, don't you?" she said. "How'd you do it?"

Miles couldn't tell her the truth. He compromised and offered what amounted to the truth. "By becoming another human being," he said, "I just dropped everything I had been—"

"Maybe it's easier for a man," she said.

Her name was Dorothy. "Dot—everybody calls me," she said. "The last name doesn't matter—I've had plenty of them." He told her his name was Michael Fowler. "I bet nobody ever called you Mike," she said.

He assured her that she was wrong but didn't tell her that was what the bartenders of Camden had called him. That and professor.

"Why not?" he asked.

"I don't know—you're too grand for Mike."

Grand! In his hospital pajamas and the awful threadbare bathrobe, reeking of disinfectant. Well, everything was comparative, he supposed. "I don't want to be grand," he said earnestly. "Can't we he friends?"

The girl sighed. "You're wasting your time, fellow," she said.

"I mean it," Miles insisted, "just friends."

"Chris' knows I'll need a friend when I get out of here," the girl said, and then added cynically, realizing that he too was a patient in the charity ward, "but what can you do for me and what can I do for you?"

"We'll see," Miles said. He hadn't definitely made up his mind how far he wanted to commit himself. "What are your plans when you leave here?"

"Plans?" she said with a faint effort at a Bronx cheer. "Do you think I'd of tried to jump off the roof if I had any plans?"

"You're bound to land on your feet—you're young and pretty."

"I'm bound to land on my back, you mean. All I can do is pray for strength enough to keep sober and not get caught again."

Miles had never heard anyone talk that way before. It wasn't funny; he didn't feel like laughing. It was appalling.

"Then it's up to me," he said firmly.

"What do you mean it's up to you?"

"Well, I kept you from killing yourself so it's up to me to watch out for you."

"Thanks," she said without any enthusiasm, "but I guess you've got about all you can do to take care of yourself, brother."

"We'll both be out of here in a day or two," Miles said. "Where are you going? You must have some friends."

"Sure, I've got friends. They'll all slip me a drink and maybe a buck but there's no place where I can go. My girl friends all use their rooms as a place of business."

"Well, I've got money enough to take care of us for a few days," Miles said and that was as far as he committed himself that first day. "Have you any idea when you're going to be released?"

She showed more interest and animation. It was, apparently, an instinctive response to his admission that he had some money. "I'll be out in a few days," she said. "I guess they want to get rid of me—afraid I'll pull it again."

"You won't, will you?" Miles asked earnestly.

She shrugged her shoulders. "I'll take a chance," she said, "for awhile."

Why he should be so anxious to save the life of this tart and still be without regret for having killed the other one, was something he could not explain to himself. But he was formulating great plans to be of assistance to this young creature whose life he had saved.

Killing Lucy, the waif, had liberated him from Brenda. Throwing himself into the icy water had liberated him from the life of a drunken bum. He couldn't go back to that life any more than he would go back to Brenda. He wanted a new role and he saw what it was going to be. He would do something big for this girl whose life he had saved and at the same time he would keep Brenda from getting his fortune. He would do it if it led him straight to the electric chair.

But he was sure that his money, his friends, and the prestige of his family would save him from that. He was more afraid of spending the rest of his life or even the next twenty years in the penitentiary. That was the horror. But the horror was fading. His life as a bum had somehow lessened his dread of imprisonment. People weren't so bad; even the worst. There was no imprisonment worse than the imprisonment of poverty and drunkenness. Now, he felt that he probably wouldn't commit suicide even if he had the opportunity before he was arrested. Of course, he was still horrified by the thought of all the publicity and the disgrace and shame he would bring upon his family and his firm, but even that thought didn't horrify him as it once had. His sensibilities were becoming dulled. Or the instinct of self-preservation was becoming stronger.

In the meantime there was his plan for the girl. He left the hospital the same day she did and they went to Philadelphia together. He could have been discharged a few days earlier but he was told he could stay on since his bed wasn't needed and he was paying his board.

It was a shock when he saw her in street clothes. In the hospital gown and robe she had seemed childlike and pretty. Now in her cheap and vulgar clothes she was something different or rather she was what she said she was—the discarded mistress of a racketeer. She was young but not childlike. Young and whorish; yes, definitely whorish.

But he caught a glimpse of himself in a mirror and realized that he was probably equally disillusioning to the girl. After all, she had told him what she was and what to expect but he hadn't told her anything. He had sent out for a cheap ready-made suit—the filthy rags he had worn when he jumped from the coal docks had been burned. But the girl complimented him.

"You're younger than I thought you was," she said and for the first time it seemed to Miles there was less despair in her voice.

They both felt rather weak by the time they arrived in Philadelphia. The girl said she was jittery and needed a drink. But Miles didn't want to go to a saloon or any public place in Philadelphia. Of course many weeks had passed but they would still be on the lookout for him, although he doubted if he would he recognized—he was so thin and emaciated.

The girl was resourceful. "I know a good clean place," she said, "where we can rent an apartment for a day, a week, or a month. They're completely furnished for housekeeping."

"But we'll probably go on to New York in a few days," Miles pointed out.

"We can take it by the day. I think I can get it for two dollars—at the most two and a half."

"You're anxious to stay in Philadelphia awhile?" Miles suggested.

"Yes—that is just long enough to gather up a few clothes I left with a girl friend."

"You're sure it's a girl friend?" Miles asked.

"Of course I'm sure. You don't think I ever want to see that guy again, do you?"

"I don't know," Miles said. "Do you?"

"Even if I did," the girl went on, explaining her code, "I wouldn't do it while I was with you. I wouldn't two-time you that way."

"You're under no obligation to me," Miles said quickly.

"Don't you worry about that guy. That's all finished. Come on—we'll take the subway here and that'll take us right out to the apartment I've been telling you about."

They rode for about twenty minutes on the subway and then Miles waited in a corner drug store while Dot went to rent the apartment. He didn't want to take part in the transaction. She returned in about five minutes. He had bought a *Saturday Evening Post* and was drinking a coca-cola. It seemed natural to be doing these casual middle-class things again. During his weeks in Camden he hadn't read a line.

The apartment, just around the corner, consisted of two rooms, complete with brass bed, overstuffed furniture, red and yellow cretonne drapes, and a gas plate in the bathroom.

"Nice, isn't it?" Dot asked as she triumphantly led him through the horror.

Miles looked at her. Her expression was completely serious.

"Yes," he said, "very nice." He preferred the ten-dollar-a-month room he had occupied in Camden.

"And I got it for two dollars a day," Dot said proudly. "Twelve by the week—if we stay a week, we won't have to pay for the last day."

"We won't stay a week," Miles said with conviction. He took off his coat and dropped wearily into a chair.

Maternally, the girl noticed the let-down. "You look all tired out," she said. "You lie down on the divan while I go out and rustle some liquor and some food."

Miles obeyed. He did feel exhausted. He stretched out on the hideous divan. Then he sat up again and took a ten-dollar bill from his pocket. He handed it to the girl. "Will that be enough?"

She laughed. "That would be enough for a week. I won't lay in much stuff if we're only going to stay a day or so. Shall I get gin or rye or Scotch or what?"

"Get what you like," Miles said, dropping back full length on the divan again. "I don't think I'll take anything—or not more than one drink anyway."

"I'll just get one bottle then," the girl said. "I need a couple to pick me up. I don't seem to get accustomed to anything except gin," she apologized. "You see I started on gin."

Miles smiled. "By all means get gin then," he said.

Apparently, she would not even indulge her own tastes without consulting the man who was footing the bills.

She bent down and kissed him. It was their first affectionate exchange. Miles didn't know whether he found it pleasant or not.

"I'll be right back," she said from the doorway, "but you take a nap if you can."

But he wasn't sleepy. When her footsteps had died away, he jumped up and looked in the mirror. The mark of her cheap lipstick was visible on his chin. He carefully removed it with his new five cent pocket handkerchief. He had an impulse to leave a twenty dollar bill on the table and hurry away.

He was a fool to trust this girl. Probably, she was already at the telephone trying to get her faithless lover. Or the police. Miles was sure she suspected he was a fugitive from justice, although, of course, she had no idea what his crime had been. But he doubted if she were calling the police. She had been tutored in a school where the one unforgivable sin is to squeal. Even when she had been almost killed by an abortionist and left to the mercy of a charity hospital, she had refused to give the name of the man responsible. No, she might be telephoning to her lover but Miles felt sure she was not notifying the police. Perhaps, she wouldn't come back at all. Ten dollars was a great deal of money to a girl of that sort. Maybe it was just as well. But Miles felt reasonably sure that she would return.

He stretched out on the divan again. Perhaps he did doze, for in a very short time she was back, standing in the doorway, her arms full of bundles.

"Gin and groceries," she announced.

Gin and groceries! The history of an epoch. Miles hurried to take some of the bundles from her. A new sort of domestic life was starting for him.

He found that the smell of gin nauseated him. He couldn't touch it. He was sure it would have been the same with whiskey.

"I guess I saturated myself," he apologized to Dot. "You see I was blind drunk for weeks—had the d.t.'s night after night."

That was a mild exaggeration but the whole Camden episode was becoming horrible in retrospect.

"It does that to you," the girl agreed, "but you'll get over it. Don't mind if I have a few do you?"

"Not at all. Maybe a little later I'll feel differently—"

"I'll make you some coffee right away." From the small bundle she had brought from the hospital, she produced a bungalow apron and in it, she again seemed pretty and childlike.

"I want to buy you lots of pretty clothes," Miles said following the train of his thoughts.

She turned quickly. She had been measuring coffee into the pot. "You don't like my clothes?"

"I guess they're all right," Miles said hastily, "but I'd like to buy you everything new—so we really can start in on a brand new existence."

She returned to the coffee measuring. "You're a high-hat, ain't you?" she said, more a statement than a question or an accusation.

"I don't know," Miles answered. "I used to have plenty of money. Maybe I can get some of it again. Does that make me a high-hat?"

"I've heard and read about guys like you," she said, "but I've never met one before. But I knew the minute I talked to you at the hospital that you weren't a stiff."

She disappeared into the bathroom with the coffee pot. Miles heard her lighting the gas. She moved back and forth, opening cans, filling saucepans, cutting bread. There was a natural grace about her as she did those things. She lost the swishing affectations of her usual movements.

Miles, half-heartedly, offered to help. "Nothing doing," she said firmly, "you take a shut-eye and I'll wake you up to the nicest supper you've had in a long time."

She fulfilled her promise. Miles marveled that such an appetizing meal could be prepared on a two-burner stove. He was also astonished at his appetite. He couldn't remember when he had eaten such a meal. The girl was delighted but deprecated his extravagant praise. "Wait until we get a stove with an oven," she said, "and I'll fix a real meal."

She was apparently planning a future—a future for them with a full domestic flavor. Feeling rejuvenated by the excellent food, Miles found the idea not unattractive. He had no desire for solitude again.

Her drinking was moderate. She had one drink of gin, straight, as a cocktail before their meal and another with lemon and water while eating. Even after eating, Miles found the smell of the liquor repulsive and declined to join her in a gin cordial.

He insisted upon drying the dishes as she washed them.

"You've been properly brought up," she said.

Miles smiled. He didn't tell her that he had never dried dishes in his life except on camping trips when a small boy.

After everything was washed, dried, and put away, the girl refreshed her dreadful make-up and suggested a walk. Miles agreed. Some fresh air would do them good and he was sure he had nothing to fear at night in this part of the city.

Dot did not say anything but fresh air was not her objective. She led him casually but promptly to the neighborhood picture house.

"Jeez," she said, "this is the longest time in my life that I've gone without seeing a picture."

Miles didn't have the heart to refuse. The picture was one of the G-men series and it was not particularly reassuring to Miles to learn that fingerprints are infallible; that under government supervision the laxness of state and local police was rapidly disappearing; and that the Department of Justice was actually functioning in the manner of Scotland Yard. And, of course, in the manner of another great punitive force, the Canadian Mounted, they always got their men. Between these firm statements was a bristling melodrama of gunplay, swift death, captures by planes, speed boats and automobiles, and—of course—aphrodisiac episodes of passionate, but pure, love.

"It's pretty straight dope," Dot assured him; "the gangster pictures used to be the boloney but now they're not so bad."

She was thoroughly enjoying herself, holding his hand, and whispering to him the real names of the pictured overlords of the underworld. She had many phases and facets, Miles decided. Now she was a child of not more than fourteen or fifteen; in the apartment she had been an efficient housewife; that day he had saved her life against her will, she had been a savage; in bed, he was sure she would be an efficient prostitute. It all worked up, he realized, to form a composite portrait of a modern moron but he found it interesting and he was surprised by the effect of her handclasp. To her it was a casual gesture, the proper way to sit with any man who takes you to a picture show. And when Miles touched her with his knee, she did not withdraw.

"It's a grand picture, ain't it?" she said. Apparently she thought he had been emphasizing some climax on the screen. He let it go at that.

They went back to the apartment immediately after the show. Dot firmly refused his invitation to drop into a bar-room. "We've got gin and ginger-ale and plenty of sandwich stuff in the apartment," she said. Apparently, economy went with her domestic efficiency. She had brought him more than five dollars change from the ten dollar bill and he had been amazed that she could have bought that much food, to say nothing of the gin, for less than five dollars. He had insisted that she put the change in her purse. At first she had refused half-heartedly but she admitted that she was entirely penniless and finally accepted the money—"if you're sure you can spare it." He was sure.

They picked up some oranges for breakfast. Dot had forgotten them. In fact, oranges were not a necessary part of her breakfast but she realized that Miles belonged to the orange-juice-and-toast class. Miles remembered the bum who couldn't eat anything early in the morning except doughnuts.

Back in the apartment, which was not quite so dreadful at night due to the economy of the electric-light wattage, Dot had a gin and ginger-ale and Miles had an appetizing sandwich and a ginger-ale without gin.

Dot yawned. "Gee, the hospital gets you into bad habits, don't it? What do you say we hit the hay?"

The two rooms were separated only by an archway curtained with the dreadful cretonne. She went into the bedroom, inspected the linen on the brass bed, beat the pillows briskly, and turned down the covers. The action was not suggestively sensual; it was merely domestic.

She returned, undoing the snappers on her dress. "Another sandwich?" she asked.

"No thanks," Miles said and then mumbled: "I'll sleep on the divan in here; you take the bed."

She was seeking a tucked-away snapper. Surprised by Miles' pronouncement she abandoned the search.

"How come?" she asked.

Almost abstractedly, Miles went over and found the missing snapper for her, just as if he had known where it was all the time. He had always done things of that sort for Brenda but he had not been thinking about Brenda. It was entirely an involuntary action.

"Listen, child," he said; "I want to help you if I can; I've had a damn' worthless life—so far. And you can be my friend—I'm afraid of being alone again. But that doesn't mean we have to sleep together. I'm—I'm not demanding your body."

It sounded very silly and melodramatic as he said it but to the girl, with her motion-picture ideas and ideals, it sounded very nice and just right. She listened carefully.

Her dress, finally completely unsnapped, fell to the floor. "What's the matter with me?" she said. "What's the matter with my body?"

Miles blushed. "Nothing," he said and immediately realized that was an understatement. It was a beautiful body. There wasn't the slightest indication that an abortionist had performed almost deadly work on it.

She went over and put her arm around his shoulder. "You're the strangest guy I've ever met and I've met plenty."

"All right then, I'm strange," Miles said, "and maybe it's part of my strangeness that I don't want a girl who's still in love with another man."

"I'm not," she denied, without releasing him. "And if I was? Girls like me are used to loving one man and sleeping with another. The men we love make us do that. And we don't mind. When your money runs out, we won't go hungry—not if I have to hustle on the streets—I'm glad now you saved my life. Honest I am—"

"So you can walk the streets for me!" He was greatly moved. It was the most astonishing thing any woman had ever said to him. He vaguely realized that she was trying to tell him that sleeping with him was just a gesture but she was willing to do much more than that and it was a tribute not an insult.

"You're the finest woman I've ever met," he said and he meant it.

"Now you're kidding me," she said, untying his dime store four-in-hand. "Don't do it. We know what it's all about. Don't let's slice boloney except for sandwiches. I'm not in love with you. I hope to Christ I never fall again but you're a swell guy and maybe I can appreciate you. Anyway, I can only live with a man one way. . . . I don't believe in any other way. . . . I couldn't be bothered . . . and it wouldn't be natural."

"You're dead right," Miles agreed. He didn't tell her that he'd never been natural—that he'd been a damned perverted slave to a vile woman.

She modestly went into the bathroom and let him undress in privacy. Almost half an hour passed before she returned, wearing a rather crumpled yellow nightie which, apparently, had also been in the bundle she had brought from the hospital.

"Since reading them ads," she explained as she switched out the light, "I always wash my undies before I go to bed. I can't sleep if I don't."

Six

By morning, there was no doubt in Miles' mind that he was going to attempt to go through with his plan. Dot hadn't asked a question. That was one of the things that endeared her to him. He was sure she was normally inquisitive but she kept her curiosity under restraint. He didn't realize that that trait had been beaten into her. The first thing the sweetheart of a racketeer must learn is to ask no questions. She told him that later when he complimented her on her silence.

"Nine o'clock," she said, springing out of bed. Miles had no idea how she knew it was nine o'clock. Neither of them had a watch. An outside bell must have rung somewhere.

"Now don't you move," she said, pulling on the bungalow apron over the yellow nightie. "I'll have breakfast ready in fifteen minutes."

Miles felt very luxurious. "I'll take my bath," he said.

She giggled. "You can't bathe while I'm fixing breakfast," she pointed out.

Miles understood. Sleeping with him was all right but it would be vulgar to watch him bathe while she made the coffee. Brenda walked through the apartment at any hour of the day or night without a stitch on but she seldom would sleep with him.

Miles turned over and stretched. He remained in bed until the delicious smell of the coffee and the crisping bacon brought him to his feet with cheers. He dressed quickly.

At the breakfast table, he confided his plan to her. "I've got about a hundred dollars left," he said.

She was astonished. "That's a lot of jack these days," she said earnestly. "I'm surprised that the hospital let you get away with that much."

"They were very, very decent," Miles said, "and some day I want to give them some money—but now I want it for you. A hundred dollars isn't as much as I want to spend on one dress for you."

"Go on! I ain't got no big ideas. I'd rather have ten dresses at ten dollars than one for a hundred. I like lots of changes and bright colors."

"You'll have ten at a hundred!" Miles promised recklessly. "If—"

She laughed as she poured more coffee. There was always an "if."

"Anyway," Miles went on, "a hundred dollars is plenty to get us to New York. I've got quite a lot of cold cash in a safe deposit vault. I've got lots of other things too but I won't try to get anything else. But I've been thinking and there's one chance in a hundred that I might be able to get the money; the man at the vaults might not know me or might not remember that the police were after me months ago. Or he might be some underpaid wretch who'll take a tip for not noticing me."

"That's about the size of it," Dot agreed. "If he gets a cut on what you take out, he'll be plenty forgetful."

"I hadn't thought about that," Miles said, "that's a good business-like idea—ten percent of what I take out. Of course, my wife may have gotten a court order to let her get in the box but I doubt it—I think more time would have to elapse."

Then followed the perfectly natural question. "What are they after you for?" the girl asked.

"Does it matter?"

"Not to me. Forget it. I'm sorry I mentioned it."

"That's all right," Miles assured her. "You'll have to know, sooner or later, but I'd rather not talk about it now."

"Okay, Mike. Forget it—"

"If I get the money," Miles went on, "we'll be refugees and if they get me it may go tough with you for a little while—"

"Say, I've been third-degree'd before," the girl interrupted; "but they've never gotten anything out of me yet—the bastards—except a free lay—"

Miles was becoming accustomed to her little outbursts. Nevertheless he was glad to take refuge for a second in his cup of coffee.

"If we get the money," he said, "we'll have plenty of fun before they get me. If I don't get it—if the clerk or the guard turns me over to the police—well, that's my bad luck but you'll have all the money you'll ever need."

"Listen," she said from the deep well of her experience, "they'll never let you get away with a dime; they've probably got it by now."

Miles realized she misunderstood the nature of his crime. "It's my money," he said. "I didn't steal anything."

"Then you've got nothing to worry about," she said. "If you've got coin and have paid your income tax and ain't kidnapped nobody there ain't nothing a lawyer can't fix for you."

"No," Miles said, "if they get me, there's nothing left for me to do except to make my will."

She understood immediately and passed the bacon to show that everything was still all right. "You're the last person in the world I'd think would bump off a guy but you never can tell. But I still say they can get you off if you've got enough jack—"

"Maybe you're right. I certainly didn't mean to kill her."

Now she was surprised and made no effort to conceal it. "You bumped off a dame! Your wife?"

Miles shook his head. How foolish of him to have blurted it out that way. "I was crazy drunk," he said. "I killed her instead of my wife."

"I'm getting it all now," she said; "that's why you can't touch liquor. Jeez! That is bad business but I can see the answer. They'll say you was crazy and just leave off the drunk part of it. And then your jumping off the dock in Camden just fits in with it. You get that Jewish lawyer—what's his name—or that other guy out in Chicago. And I'll be able to help. I'll say how funny you act every now and then, like wanting to take a bath when I fry bacon and how I get afraid of you—"

"But you're not, are you?" Miles asked quickly.

She laughed heartily. Then she leaned across the table and kissed him. "Sure I'm afraid of you. 'Bout half as much as I'm afraid of a mouse." And then she quickly added, as if it were a choice witticism; "but believe me, if I ever see you with a drink in your hand, I'll start moving."

He looked at her in complete, almost shocked amazement. He didn't dream that anyone could he so flippant about murder. It had never bothered his conscience or his dreams but he hadn't been flippant or casual about it and he always considered that if they did get him, they would be perfectly justified in electrocuting him. He had even decided what he would order for his last meal and wondered if they would let him have a gramophone in the death cell so he would play his favorite music: the last act of "Götterdämmerung."

But here was a woman who apparently considered murder—or at any rate this murder—just an unpleasant incident of a drunk; like falling downstairs or breaking a glass. Fortunately, she did not realize how she had shocked him. She began gathering together the dishes. "I'll be cleaning up if we're going to New York," she said.

"It only takes two hours on the train," Miles said.

"A bus is a lot cheaper," she pointed out.

But now that Miles had definitely made up his mind, he didn't want to fool around with busses and petty economies. "No," he said, "we'll take the train."

"Well, anyway," the girl said, continuing her brisk scraping, "I want to get out of here before noon so the landlady don't try to collect for any extra time."

Miles realized it was going to be difficult to make this girl extravagant even if he secured possession of all his money and properties. He managed to talk her out of reclaiming her few possessions from the friend who was keeping them for her. No matter what happened now, he'd have plenty of money and she could buy whatever she needed. Since he'd made up his mind, he hated any delays. Dot reluctantly consented. She wanted her own things but she supposed she could send for them or, since it was only a two-hour trip, she could come back for them. Miles gladly agreed to that. She'd probably change her mind in New York.

On the train, he decided it would be foolish to go to the bank without first definitely learning his status. After all, there was always the possibility that he had not been identified as the murderer. Of course it was a very remote possibility but it was a possibility. He realized that detectives in fact are often not as clever (or for that matter as stupid) as they are in fiction. But when he considered the coincidence of his disappearance on the day of the murder and all the other bits of evidence, it seemed extremely unlikely that he was not being sought.

He bought a New York paper—the first he had seen since the day of the murder. Of course, there was no mention of the crime or the refugee. It would have been surprising if there had been. Miles realized that even a murder by a Farrington, of the Long Island and Park Avenue Farringtons, couldn't hold the public interest for more than four months, unless, of course, new clues were constantly being developed. But what new clues could there be? They hadn't located him and that was all there was to it. Of course, there probably had been hundreds of false clues. He hated to think how many men had probably been arrested as Miles Farrington in various parts of the world.

He read the society notes and gossip columns very carefully. There might be some mention of Brenda but there wasn't—not a word. There were many items about his friends. The Deans were going to Europe; the Castles were returning. Practically everyone was in Palm Beach or returning from there. His cousins were entertaining and being entertained. Apparently the stigma of the name had not overwhelmed them. Why should it? They had never been close. After the death of his parents, Miles had practically severed all connections with relatives. They all hated Brenda and thought Miles a fool.

Miles did notice, however, that none of his closest friends or his business partners was named in any of the lists. He hoped it was only a coincidence. He hated to think of them, especially his partners, figuratively bowing their heads for him. They had always been loyal to him in spite of the fact that they too hated Brenda and thought him the chump of chumps—the ultimate chump of all times. Perhaps they were right.

He decided as the train pulled out of Trenton (he thought of the Princeton boy who probably had been a link in the chain of evidence against him) that it would be foolish for him to go to the library and search the newspaper files. There was probably always a detective on duty at the public library. He would send Dot and caution her not to ask for the papers of the particular day he wanted but to request the issues of the whole week or better still the month.

He confided his change of plans to Dot and she agreed that it was a good idea. It was silly to go to the bank and offer the guy a big cut when he mightn't have the faintest idea what it was all about. They hadn't been able to get a train immediately and it was too late to go to the bank that day.

They discussed the question of a hotel. The mid-day train was not crowded and their part of the day coach was almost empty. There was no danger of being overheard. It was a great relief to have someone with whom he could discuss all these things. For months he had been forced to decide everything for himself.

Should they go to a hotel in Newark, Brooklyn, or New York? Miles was for throwing caution to the winds, staking everything on one bold stroke and decided on New York—a small hotel somewhere. Did Dot know one? Dot knew several but she thought it was a bad idea. She believed in going where the crowds are thickest. Without even going into the street, they could go from the station into the Hotel Pennsylvania.

Yes, she knew they couldn't register without baggage but there was a place in the station, several places in fact—downstairs and up in the part that led out to the street—where a suitcase could be bought. Miles agreed that the idea seemed as good as any. He couldn't remember that he had ever known anyone in the Hotel Pennsylvania and he hadn't been in the place very many times.

"It doesn't matter if anybody does know you," Dot said; "they won't see you. We go into the hotel—we get a room—I beat it to the library—that'll be a novelty for little Dot—you take that bath you missed this morning.

When I get back, if it's the bad news, you hold everything. We don't even have the bell-boy or the waiter up. I bring you in sandwiches and Java; in the morning we take a taxi to the bank. You do or you don't. If you do, we're out of town on the first train. Anything wrong with that?"

"It's perfect," Miles said heartily. "You're wonderful."

And he meant it. Excitement was in his blood again. The chase was on.

At first, things moved without a hitch. On the lower level of the station, in a men's shop, they bought a nondescript leather suitcase for a few dollars. Again Dot proved the superior mind. Miles said anything would do—the cheapest one they had. He thought of the magnificent one he had checked in the station months before; the police must have had that for a long time.

But Dot quickly vetoed the idea of the cheapest bag. A straw one would be out of place in the Pennsylvania; bell-hops would notice it. And because they only had one bag, Miles should carefully say to the clerk they'd only be there one night. She put her bundle into the suitcase but even with it and all the newspapers they had, it felt very light. However, they decided to take a chance on it. You can't find a brick in the middle of the Pennsylvania Station.

They were assigned to a room at six dollars and the clerk seemed disinterested in the length of their stay, although his disinterest was very polite. The bell-boy seemed equally disinterested in the quality or weight of their suitcase and grateful, with the days of the depression still upon him, for the quarter tip.

Miles wanted to order a rickey for Dot but, thirsty as she was, she wouldn't think of it. Nobody was coming in that room until she was back from the library and she'd be on her way as soon as she removed a little railroad dirt and applied a little powder and lipstick. Miles noticed that the removal of railroad grime was a much lesser operation than the application of the lipstick and rouge.

He gave her definite instructions. She was to look for the report of three things—the murder, the disappearance of Miles Farrington, and Brenda. The chances were that all these things would be in one story but maybe not; maybe not.

He didn't give her the details of the crime but he described the girl, the circumstances and the name of the hotel. Certainly from that she could put two and two together. Of course she wouldn't arrive at the motive but Miles Farrington had never been able to explain that to himself.

Her loyalty didn't waver for a second. She kissed him when she left. "It was some other guy," she said cheerfully.

She took some of the generous amount of stationery provided by the hotel and would buy a pencil at the drug store. Sure, she'd take a taxi going and coming back. Of course, she had plenty of money. She had all that change he'd given her yesterday. He hadn't seen her spend any of it, had he? Yes, she had spent one nickel in the station toilet in Philadelphia. He liked the brusque way she veered away from sentimentality. He kissed her again and told her he didn't care what news she brought back, just so she came back as quickly as possible. She promised. She wouldn't even go to the dime store and God knows she needed things.

This time he felt no temptation to run away before she returned. But the time seemed interminable. They hadn't thought to bring in any reading matter. He just couldn't sit in that room and look out on the court for the hour or two that must elapse before she would return. He violated her instructions and went down into the lobby for papers and magazines. He left a note saying he would he back immediately in case she should return before he did. But the note was there and the room empty when he returned with the afternoon papers and a liberal supply of weeklies.

But after he had glanced at the papers and looked at the cartoons in *The New Yorker,* he discovered he couldn't read, he had the feeling he had read that *Nation* before although he hadn't seen a copy in months. He was too nervous to read. He was sure she had been gone for more than an hour. He had figured on an hour as the minimum time but realized it might take her longer. He hadn't been able to settle on a maximum time. He turned on the radio and although he could find nothing to hold his attention, he kept it on in lieu of a watch.

He decided he was hungry and disobeyed Dot's instructions again. He ordered tea and a sandwich. The waiter looked familiar to Miles and he had a bad moment but apparently the recognition was not mutual. In fact, after the man had been generously tipped, he genially asked Miles how he liked New York. The fellow must have worked at some restaurant or club where he used to eat, Miles decided. It didn't occur to him that he might have reached the jittery stage where everyone seemed familiar.

The quarter hours chimed off endlessly on the radio but Dot didn't return. Every time he heard the elevator stop he became tensely expectant but the footsteps always went past his door or down a different corridor. It was getting dark in the court. Miles became worried, tried to reassure himself, and finally was frantic. Something must have happened. Either a traffic accident or she had been arrested at the library. In the latter event, although they had not discussed that possibility, Miles felt sure she would not give his name. It would be her code to remain stubbornly silent. If there had been an accident, she certainly would notify him, as she knew they had registered as Mr. and Mrs. Michael Fowler.

It was much worse than when he had been roaming the streets, expecting a heavy hand to fall upon his shoulder at any moment. He could at least drop into saloons and mingle with people. But this staying in a hotel room with only a blank court to look at was an inquisition of a peculiar, dreadful sort. Just at the moment when he decided he couldn't bear it for another second, she appeared. She was bearing gifts—a box of cheap candy and the afternoon papers. Miles was so glad to see her that for the first time he almost broke down.

"I didn't dream how long I'd been," she explained, "until I came out into the street and saw it was dark. It took me so long and I had to wait and wait; you needn't worry about being nabbed for asking for back papers. It seemed just hundreds of people had the very papers I wanted."

"There was so much to copy?" Miles ventured, hoping to get her back on the main thread. He was sure she wasn't deliberately torturing him. She was just talking in her usual rambling fashion.

"There wasn't anything to copy," she said; "that's what took me so long. I read and read and read—up one column and down another—but except for two or three tiny little items—I've got them here—there wasn't a thing—"

She looked around the room. "You've been a bad boy; you've gotten papers and have been eating—"

"I just couldn't stand the strain."

"Well, it's all right—"

"But there must have been some big story about—about the murder. What about the tabloids?"

"You didn't kill her," Dot said almost contemptuously. "I couldn't believe it even when you told it to me yourself. You couldn't kill anybody, honey."

"I didn't kill her?" But that was incredible. It was not only that she had been blue and cold with death but he remembered feeling for her heart beats, frantically but carefully. No one had ever been more completely dead; more beyond any hope of resuscitation. There wasn't a pulmotor in the world could have brought that girl back to life. If she hadn't been dead, then he had been insane, absolutely insane. And still was. "She wasn't dead?" he asked.

"Oh yeah, she was dead all right," Dot explained, "but there was just a little teeny-weeny item. It said she died from natural causes—the maid discovered the body when she went in to clean the room—"

Natural causes! Well, murder was a natural cause. But he had killed that girl. He had choked her to death as she squirmed and struggled, his strong frame holding her emaciated body powerless beneath him. She hadn't died of fright or a heart attack. She had fought with all her strength, which had been very slight.

"But what did the papers say about her husband? What about the man who registered with her? The man who ran away, leaving a dead woman in the bed? Even if they thought she died from natural causes, they must have known she had been dead for hours. And the man had left her dead. What did the papers say about him?"

The questions just burst out, his words falling over each other. Dot was surprised. She had never seen him so excited. But she remained placid.

"I've been thinking and thinking," she said. "Either you was so tight that you imagined the whole thing—"

"But the paper did say that the girl was found dead," Miles pointed out.

"Yeah, that's so; then it must have been the other thing I thought of. That hotel is owned by a bunch of racketeers. Way-ups. Cheater Malone is the head of them—"

"Yes, I heard that. That's why I went there with her."

"And lucky you did, fellow. Well, Cheater was in a peck of trouble already and he couldn't afford to get in any more. He and his mob must have figured if the stink of a big murder in the hotel got out, they were just about washed up, so they moved the body into a single room—the papers said she had registered alone and they had identified her from letters found in her pocketbook—"

"Yes, I think she did have some letters," he said.

"Well, so they put her in a single room, get a certificate from one of their doctors—they got plenty of them—or buy one from a police doctor and let it go at that."

"Maybe they thought it was a natural death," Miles interrupted. "There weren't any signs of violence that I could see."

"All the more reason why they'd move her into a single room. They wouldn't want it known that a streetwalker had registered with a guy who took it on the lam when she died. After all, that hotel is an expensive joint, not a flop house, and hasn't a bad reputation out of town. And there are a lot of decent theatrical people living there. It's right on the street with all them theatres."

"And you think maybe—maybe they don't even know I was there? I mean, they didn't discover the real name of the man who registered with her?"

"I don't believe anybody knows that but you and me, honey," Dot said, carelessly. "Of course, maybe they did find out just for their own satisfaction; but why should they go snooping around? They'd only attract attention to the hotel. They couldn't keep a story like that out of the papers. No, my bet is they wanted the thing hushed up as quickly as possible and they spent plenty to do it."

"They certainly seem to have done it."

"And how! Only three papers had a word about it and they just had a few measly sentences—not a picture or nothing."

"It's incredible!" Then he had another thought. "What about my disappearance? Didn't that get any publicity either?"

"Not one tiny word—I went up one column and down another. I went through the papers twice, thinking maybe the first time I had been so anxious to find the murder I might have forgotten the other things. They all had little pieces about Mrs. Farrington arriving in Reno by plane. Here, I'll read you the one that had the most—the *Journal*. 'Reno, Nev.—Mrs. Miles Farrington of New York City arrived by plane today for the purpose of establishing a residence and securing a divorce from her husband, Miles Farrington. . . . Then it says where you live and who your parents were and your business but you know all that so I didn't copy it—"

"Go on," Miles begged.

"'Mr. Farrington could not be located at his apartment or in his office,'" she read on; "'an employee of the firm said Mr. Farrington was out of town for an indefinite stay but no member of the firm would make any statement or allow himself to be quoted.'"

Miles smiled. That was so typical of the office and his partners. But what could they be thinking now? And what action had they taken?

"You read through the papers right up until today?"

"Every single paper. It's more reading than I ever done in my life and I don't care if I never see another newspaper."

"And there wasn't anything more about Mrs. Farrington's divorce?"

"Not a line."

"That's funny—she's surely had time to get it by now."

The whole thing was completely phantastic and incredible. Miles decided it was useless to try and figure it out. His partners would have to put the pieces together for him. He reached for the telephone and then decided against that. There was too much to talk about. He would wait until morning and go to the office.

"It's lucky we thought about the papers," Dot prattled on. "Now you won't have to give anything to the man at the bank, will you?"

"I won't have to get that money," Miles explained; "I can draw checks. If nobody knows what happened, everything is just as it was except that I've got more money. I've saved more money in the last months than I ever did in my life—just by not spending any."

"Well, let's spend a little now," Dot suggested. "I'm awfully hungry. And we don't have to lay low any more, do we?"

"No," Miles said, "except that I'd rather not see anyone I know tonight."

He took out his money and counted it. There was seventy-six dollars and some odd change. "All I need is taxi fare to the office in the morning," he said; "the rest we'll spend tonight."

"You're nuts," Dot said. "How could we spend all that?" She was fooling with the radio. "Nothing but talk . . . talk . . . talk!"

Miles thought she meant him. "I'm sorry, honey," he apologized, "I know you must be—"

She laughed. "I was talking about the radio, you old funny," she explained. "I'd like to hear some good hot music."

Although there were probably hundreds of places where he could have dined without meeting anyone he knew, he was glad to have an excuse for eating in their room. He tried not to think that it was because he was ashamed to go into a good dining room with Dot, in the present state of her make-up and attire. God knows, his own appearance was funny enough. Now that he was Miles Farrington again, the twelve-fifty suit became almost a theatrical costume or something for a fancy dress ball.

He ordered every delicacy on the bill of fare and the finest champagne for Dot. In spite of the fact that this should be a night of supreme celebration, Miles still found he couldn't take a drink. The champagne was very nice, Dot said, but Miles noticed she had difficulty in finishing the pint. He was sure she would have preferred gin.

But he sympathized with her. All the delicacies he had ordered did not tempt his palate. He just nibbled at them. His excuse was that the tea and sandwiches had ruined his appetite. It seemed incredible that a few short months should change the viewpoint and habits of a lifetime but he couldn't get the thought of his Camden days out of his mind—the days when he had lived on free lunch and handouts because he didn't want to waste his money on food. The guinea hen gagged him when he thought of that. How long would it take to forget? He realized that he mustn't get morbid and feel sorry for himself. Sorry for himself! A murderer, whose crime had been covered up without any effort or intent on his part!

"You're worrying again," Dot said with her usual penetration; "gee, honey, there's nothing to worry about now—is there?"

"No, of course not," Miles agreed; "it's just a hangover."

"But you haven't had a thing to drink," Dot pointed out.

In spite of their extravagance, the guinea hen and the champagne, the dinner check was considerably less than a twenty dollar bill; so much less that, when Miles waved away the change, the waiter was obviously astonished and Dot distressed.

But she recovered quickly. "I know what we're going to do," she said brightly, "we're going to a picture show."

"Gee, I'd rather not," Miles mildly objected. "I might just run into somebody and I don't want to take the risk of my partners knowing I'm back before I see them."

It wasn't good enough. "We can take a taxi to Fourteenth Street; there are lots of pictures down there to choose from and you certainly won't see a soul you know down there. There are so many pictures I want to see. I missed so many when I was having my trouble."

Miles couldn't refuse her and to Fourteenth Street they went. He dimly realized as he sat through a dull picture, Dot firmly clasping his hand, that he had entered into a strange servitude; and a future of nightly picture shows was almost as ghastly as a past of nightly drinking in filthy saloons. But back in the hotel room with the girl in his arms, he forgot all about that and decided she was a swell kid.

Seven

For the first time since the murder, Miles did not feel the hot breath of the pursuing police; and the menacing hand, which he always conceived as about to fall on his shoulder, had never been raised. And also for the first time since the murder, Miles was unable to sleep. His mind was too full of if's and and's.

He considered the possibility of a trap but rejected it. He had never heard of a case where the police had been able to conceal a murder in order to snare the murderer into their net. It was a good idea but he was sure the courts and the newspapers would not co-operate and the papers had said the girl had died a natural death. No, he was just unbelievably lucky and the beneficiary of powers above the law.

In order not to disturb Dot, he moved, sometime during the night, into the other twin bed. He fell into a troubled sleep at about daylight and only awakened when Dot, standing over him, bent down to kiss him good morning. "Walked out on me, huh?" she said.

Miles grinned up at her.

"Shall I order some breakfast?" she suggested.

Miles said that was swell and when she was at the telephone he leaped out of bed and into the bathroom. He wondered if he ought to go to the apartment first and get some human clothes but he decided against it. Brenda had probably sent his things to the club or the office. Perhaps she had returned to the apartment. There had been more than enough time for her to get a Reno divorce. But it was strange that the papers hadn't mentioned it. Perhaps it had been definitely decided that he was dead and Brenda considered a divorce unnecessary. But she couldn't be a legal widow until seven years had elapsed. Miles thought that was the New

York law. Maybe a body had been identified and buried as his. Stranger things had happened. But that surely would have been in the papers. There was always the chance that Dot had missed something. Maybe he should go to the library and check. But he decided against that. She certainly couldn't have missed the account of a murder and she had found the small item about the death of the girl—the natural death. He turned on the cold water and shut off the hot.

No, he'd wear his funny clothes to the office. It would be just one more thing to explain. In spite of his sleepless night, he had not decided what his explanation would be. First he wanted to hear what they had thought and why no public mention had been made of his disappearance. He realized that the least said the better. Fortunately, he had a reputation for reticence and he would live up to it. He would probably say that he had been very drunk (that they undoubtedly knew); that when he had been unable to persuade Brenda from going to Reno, he had gone haywire, left town, and remained drunk until, finally, he had become desperately ill. That had the advantage of being true so far as it went and wouldn't be difficult to remember.

He hurried through the elaborate breakfast which Dot had ordered. It was almost ten o'clock and he didn't want another morning to slip by. He insisted that she take all the money he had, except two dollars for taxi fare, and promised he would call her early in the afternoon. She accepted the money under protest but admitted there were a few things she must go out and buy. It was silly of him not to have let her pick up her suitcase in Philly.

"Not at all," Miles said, "and you're going to have everything new—everything. We're going on the shopping spree of a lifetime this afternoon. What time will you be back?"

"It'll only take me about an hour," Dot said. "I'll be back here at noon."

"It may take me a little longer than that," Miles explained. "There'll be so much to talk about at the office, and I'll have to go to the bank, and get some clothes."

"What's the matter with that suit?" Dot asked. "I think it looks very nice on you. If I had my iron, I could fix that shirt collar."

It was always difficult for Miles to believe that she was serious when she made remarks like that, but she was—completely serious. He kissed her affectionately. "Have a good time," he said. "And get some lunch if you get hungry—I'll call you as soon as I can."

"I'll be worried until I hear from you," she called after him and Miles realized that perhaps she would be.

In the building where he had his office, the elevator starter wasn't on duty and the boy in the car was a stranger to Miles. In fact, he wasn't recognized until he stepped into his own office. The reception clerk, who had been with them for more than five years, took one look and burst into tears. Miles was amazed and embarrassed and couldn't think of an appropriate or reassuring thing to say. He just kept pumping her hand while the usually efficient employee tried to regain her composure.

"I'll just go right on through to Mr. Sherman's office," Miles said and then changed his mind. If his return was going to be this much of a shock, maybe he'd better warn them. "No, I guess I won't," he said. "Maybe you'd better tell them I'm here—all the members of the firm who are in." Some of the partners had always been a little jealous of his friendship with George.

She tried to plug into all the offices at once. Her efforts to be business-like failed dismally. Her announcement ended in a scream. "Mr. Farrington is back! He's out here! Mr. Farrington is back!"

It was the first time he had heard his name in months. It was a shock to him. He had come to think of his name as something to be avoided, probably for the rest of his life. He expected to see detectives and police in uniform pop out of every door. Instead, his partners came on the run. They pounded him on the back; they screamed at him. They didn't burst into tears but it was evident that one or two of them were close to it. Their noise brought out the clerks and the office boys and that added to the confusion. Miles alone was calm and felt a little superior to it all.

Then they noticed his clothes and began to laugh. That relieved the tension. Miles tried to laugh with them but didn't attempt to answer any of the questions they fired at him. They wanted to take him into the board room but George Sherman intervened. George was his oldest and closest friend. It was George who had finally told him that something must be done about the open scandal of Brenda's conduct.

"Let him alone, you fellows," George said authoritatively; "can't you see he's been sick?"

The emotional greetings ended in an awkward silence. The clerks and office boys disappeared again.

"Miles is coming in with me," George Sherman went on, "and we'll have lunch together if he feels well enough."

"Sure," Miles said, "I'll be all right." It was the longest speech he had made.

George put his arm around his partner's shoulder and drew him out of the crowd. They went into George's office and Miles was affectionately pushed into a deep leather chair.

"Now you so-and-so," George said, trying to be flippant, "report!" But before Miles could say anything George quickly added: "Of course you don't have to say a damn word if you don't want to. It's enough for us—anyway enough for me—that you're back." But he couldn't refrain from adding a word of reproach: "How could you have done this to me, Miles? I've been worried to death."

"I'm sorry, George," Miles said, "very sorry. I probably don't have to tell you that I wasn't exactly responsible—I've been sick, very sick, as you guessed—"

"Amnesia? God-damn it," George Sherman swore, "I told that bunch of private detectives we hired to check every hospital in the country and Canada too—"

So detectives had been after him! Even if they had only been private detectives, Miles' vanity was restored. They hadn't found a trace of him and private detectives were supposed to be more efficient than any others.

"It wasn't exactly amnesia," he said, slowly. "I was registered under a name but not my own. I wish you'd tell me just what you did, George, and—and what Brenda did."

"I wasn't worried for a day or two," George explained. "I knew you had been terribly upset, of course. But you had several important engagements on your pad, so, finally, when I couldn't get your apartment, I called the building and they told me Brenda had gone to Reno and you hadn't been seen that day. In fact, they said the apartment was closed. That did bother me and I got in touch with Brenda—she flew out. She insisted that you were all right; that you had taken her decision very badly and were just sulking somewhere."

"She was partly right," Miles said dispassionately, "but I wasn't sulking."

"Well, I let things ride for another day. Then some checks came in that the bank had turned down—"

"Turned down! Good Lord, how much did I draw?"

"Your balance was all right but the signature was so bad the bank wouldn't cash them. Then before I called in the detectives, I did a little sleuthing on my own. When I found out how much you had drawn around the places, I really was worried. I thought somebody had knocked you on the head. Then I discovered that you had cashed a large check at the bank the next day in person."

"So you knew I was all right?"

"At first I thought so—but then I was told that there is an organized gang, clip artists they call them, who pick up drunks, rob them, and often take them to their banks and make them draw money at the point of a concealed gun."

Miles smiled. "Nothing like that . . . nobody was making me draw any money." On the contrary—the racketeer system had been his salvation, not his downfall.

"I found that out when I called in the detectives; they discovered a bartender on the West Side who knew you and had served you drinks that afternoon. He said you were alone and all right but very tight. So we decided you were on a bender and let it go at that for a couple of days and kept it out of the papers."

"And didn't notify the police?"

"No; we've been scrapping over that for weeks. The private detectives insisted they could do more if we didn't give the case to the police—of course, that's probably just part of their racket."

"And they never picked up the trail after I left the West Side saloon?"

"Apparently not—although they had a new lead every day. I was going to give them three more days—until the first, and then report the case to the police although everybody said the police wouldn't try to do anything after such a lapse of time. Most of the boys thought you must be dead but somehow I could never make myself believe it. You don't know how glad I am that my hunch was right, fellow."

"Thanks, George. And what about Brenda?"

"She's been acting up a little lately. She called off the divorce for the time being and went into Los Angeles."

"Why do you suppose she called off the divorce?"

"Well, of course she couldn't serve any papers but probably the chief reason was that she realized she'd be a damn' sight better off financially if you were dead."

"I see. Well, wire her she can go ahead and get the divorce but I won't make any settlement or give her a cent of alimony. She's had plenty."

"You're damn' right she's had and I'll do it with pleasure but she'll put up an awful squawk."

"Let her squawk. If she doesn't want a Reno divorce, I can get one in New York. She knows that."

George Sherman didn't say anything immediately. "Do you know, Miles," he finally observed, "talking to you now reminds me of the novels and the movies where the hero has an exact double—"

"'The Masquerader,'" Miles offered.

"That's one of them. I saw another one just a few weeks ago—a musical one. There have been moments since you came in here that I'm not sure I've been talking to Miles Farrington."

"Do you want me to show you that burn scar on my leg? You remember that?"

"You chump. I know damn' well it's you but you are a different person."

"An entirely different person," Miles agreed; "two or three different people."

"What'll I tell the boys? And how on earth have you lived all these months on five hundred dollars."

"I stayed blind drunk for weeks and then landed in the charity ward of a hospital—you don't need money in charity wards, you know. You have no idea how many people haven't any money, George."

"Gone Communist, Miles?"

"No—I haven't gone anything."

"Good! Do you feel strong enough to have lunch with the boys? And then I think you ought to go to the country or the shore for a week."

"No, I'm all right. Do you know where my things are? The boys have had their laugh at these clothes."

"I think Brenda sent everything to the club—shall I phone and make sure?"

"No, I'll go over there; you bring the gang around for lunch—my party."

"I guess there'll be an argument about that. However—And I'll get Brenda on the telephone and let you know—"

"You needn't let me know," Miles said. "There's nothing to discuss. She can take it or leave it—a divorce in Reno for her or one in New York for me."

"Now that's the new Miles talking!"

"Like him?"

"And how! Boy, haven't I been trying to make you do it for ten years or more? And it took a big drunk and a spell of sickness—well, it's worth it—I think."

That was far from the truth but Miles made no denial. Strange, how the story made sense, completely dropping the one important, motivating thing—the murder; the murder that had been the purge and had created a new Miles Farrington.

He only vaguely, as if from a distance, heard George say: "Then I'll just tell the boys you stayed on a bender until you landed in the alcoholic ward and they're to ask no questions."

"They may ask anything they like," Miles said, knowing they wouldn't ask anything important.

George pulled a decanter out of his desk. "On or off?" he asked. "I need a shot."

"I'm off it," Miles said. "It was a complete cure."

George consulted his watch. "We'll be there at one o'clock," he said. "That'll give you time for a haircut, manicure, and whatever else your soul desires." Then, hesitantly, he added: "I wish you'd let me send one of the boys with you—just to keep us from worrying."

Miles shook his head. "I give you my word, George, I won't disappear again. I'm perfectly all right; I've been all right for more than a week and, drunk or sober, I've taken care of myself for months."

"Right you are!" George agreed. "We'll be there at one."

The reception clerk shared George's worries. She just hated to see Mr. Farrington walk out of that office, alone. But Miles assured her, a bit gruffly, that he was completely recovered and in no danger of a relapse. Then he hurried away.

At the club, his reception was hearty but without frills of hysteria. After all, no word of his disappearance had leaked out. In fact, the office, he later learned, had sent out word from time to time that Mr. Farrington was away on a trip. His dues had been meticulously paid.

He was assigned a room and his trunks and bags were sent up from the store room. He waited, reading the papers and the club bulletins, while a suit was pressed.

Then he went down to the barber shop for a complete going-over. His hair had only been cut twice since he went away—once in Camden for fifteen cents and once, free, in the hospital.

Luncheon lasted two hours. It soon settled down to a business discussion as George had told the men they must not question Miles. The explanation of a prolonged drunk and subsequent amnesia—a sort of amnesia—was accepted by them as perfectly reasonable because they knew how completely unreasonable Miles had been about his harlot wife. The truth, they would not have believed under any circumstances.

Would Miles play a rubber or two of bridge after luncheon? Miles said he would be delighted. He hadn't held a card for months. He discovered that the official score had been somewhat changed and that did make him feel Rip Van Winkle-ish. George would only let him play two rubbers; then he was hurried back to the office to sign a stack of accumulated papers.

During the signing of the papers, George asked Miles how much money he would want from the cashier. Then for the first time Miles remembered Dot. He looked at his watch. It was four-thirty. Poor kid! How completely thoughtless he had been.

"I have to phone," he said, getting up out of his chair.

"Phone from here," George said. "I'll go out if it's private."

Miles was about to say he didn't want the call to go through the switchboard and then he changed his mind. He wouldn't lapse back into the old Miles.

"No," he said, sitting down again; "it's something I want you to know, George." He told the operator to get him Mrs. Michael Fowler at the Hotel Pennsylvania.

"So that's it," George said. "Well, you have my blessing, old timer."

"She's just a little gutter rat," Miles said defiantly, "but she's been wonderful to me and I'm fond of her. Not gaga about her the way I was with Brenda but fond of her."

"All right with me," George said heartily. "You were married to a lady who turned out to be a bum so you might as well reverse the process and try to make a lady out of a bum."

"I don't think I want to," Miles said. "I like her the way she is."

Dot was in tears on the telephone but after Miles talked to her for a few minutes, he decided she wasn't as much worried as she was vexed; she was a child who had been promised something and then forgotten. But she quickly cheered up and agreed to meet him anywhere he said.

"Meet me at Hattie Carnegie's," he said recklessly. "We'll just have time to buy one evening dress and then we'll go out for a real celebration."

"I'm way ahead of you," she said gleefully; "I bought a new dress."

"You did! But you didn't have money enough. How'd you manage?"

"I had money enough to buy four dresses but I didn't; I just bought one."

"But it isn't an evening dress, is it?"

"No—but it would look all right anywhere."

"Well you meet me at Carnegie's and I'm sure she'll have an evening dress you can step right into. Do you know where it is?"

"Never heard of it," Dot admitted, "but I'll find it if it's a dress shop."

"Ask them at the hotel," Miles suggested; "you got the name, didn't you?"

"I think so—Carnegie like the public library."

"That's it and have you money enough for the taxi?"

"I've got money enough to make a down payment on one."

Miles was beginning to notice that the girl couldn't respond to a simple question with a simple answer. She had to make an observation of some sort—usually a wise-crack. However, most of them, he thought, were pretty cute. He decided as he disconnected that actually she was the clinging vine type. Nature had never intended her to be promiscuous and that was why her love affairs had turned out so badly.

George had diplomatically stepped out of the office when Miles was connected with Dot. He did not return immediately. Miles was not sure of the location of the Carnegie shop although he knew that Brenda bought most of her clothes there and that he paid bills of a thousand dollars and more, month after month. He found the address in the telephone book.

He was just about to call the cashier when George came back into the room. He had a small pocket check book for Miles and five hundred dollars in bills. "Think this will see you through the first round?" he asked.

Miles grinned. "Well, I have to make up for lost time," he said, stuffing the money into his pocket without counting it.

"Where's your wallet?" George asked.

Miles shrugged his shoulders. Where indeed? "Everything's gone," he said, "but my trunk is full of 'em." What must that janitor have thought when he discovered all that junk among the incinerator ashes? Possibly, in fact, probably, nothing had ever been discovered. Other ashes had piled on top of those and the whole lot eventually hauled away. Everything was taking on a different aspect now that he realized only private detectives had been in pursuit.

He reached for his hat. "I've got to run along, George," he said. "I shouldn't have left her all day—she's worried about me."

"That's swell. It's time you're having somebody worry about you."

Still Miles hesitated. "I can't tell you how sorry I am George," he said. "I mean—not to have dropped you a line or—or anything."

"I'll never understand it," George said, equally serious. "But as long as you came through all right forget it."

"You'll just have to believe that I was crazy or just plain crazy. You see, for a while I thought I'd never come back—never again see anyone I'd ever known."

"That's what I was afraid of—I guess I know you pretty well, Miles, different as we are."

Miles didn't say anything.

"There's only one thing and then it's all over unless you bring it up," George said. "If you let another woman, legally or otherwise, get to you the way Brenda did, I'll do something drastic."

"I never will," Miles promised, "and if I do, just put me out of my misery."

"I'll do that," George said. "See you in the morning."

Eight

Miles had a moment of old-time squeamishness in the cab, going to East Forty-ninth Street. What would the employees of Hattie Carnegie think of Miles Farrington appearing to buy an evening frock for a girl who was, obviously—well, obviously what she was.

The mood quickly passed. What the hell difference did it make what the saleswomen or Miss Carnegie, herself, thought, so long as he had good money to pay for what he bought!

Anyway, Dot had said she had bought a new dress. It was probably more violent than the one she had been wearing but, at least, it would be clean. He reached the shop first and after carefully looking inside waited on the sidewalk. He was there for about fifteen minutes before she arrived and then not in a cab but hurrying along from Fifth Avenue.

"They told me," she said, breathlessly, now like a small child expecting to be scolded, "that I could get a bus right across from the hotel that would bring me right here. And it did, too, but it took forever. I could have walked."

Miles kissed her gently. "I want you to ride in taxis," he said, "until I get you a car of your own."

She held open her coat so he could see the dress underneath. It was a very severe dark blue dress, with a white shirred collar and a white patent-leather belt.

"It's lovely," Miles said, enthusiastically and truthfully. "Where'd you get it?"

"Klein's and I knew you'd like it. I look like I was back in the convent only I never was there but I used to see the girls pass on Eutaw Place in Baltimore. You men are all alike. In public you want a girl to dress like she was in mourning for her grandmother but in bed you want her to be a bitch in heat."

"Anyway, it's very becoming," Miles said, taking her arm and leading her into the shop. He offered her cigarettes—the special club package. She noticed it.

"High-hat cigarettes," she said. And then quite casually she asked: "Is everything all right?"

"Everything is perfect."

The saleswoman in command did not seem at all surprised that a young lady wearing a fifteen dollar coat, trimmed with cat, and one of Klein's cheaper models, should be asked to choose from three of Miss Carnegie's finer (and needless to say more expensive) evening models.

"Take all three of them," Miles suggested but Dot immediately and emphatically said she wouldn't think of it and Miles realized it probably was better for them to get settled in an apartment before she started on her shopping campaign in earnest.

He knew which of the three frocks she really liked the best, although he could see she wanted him to make the choice. His selection was a fragile affair of pale yellow with silver cut-outs. The saleswoman was pushing a blue affair and Miles was sure she would get a premium if she sold it. It was dowdy. Dot had picked a wide-flowing frock of velvet in lavender tones with splashes of orange.

The saleswoman was patient but superior. "Don't you think this one is more suited to you?" She referred to the blue.

Dot was intimidated. Miles went to her rescue.

"I think you're right," he said to the saleswoman, "but this is to be for a very gala night and so I think probably the purple one will be better—it's gayer."

"I like it much better," Dot said quickly and the transaction was closed.

He drew out his check book. "I've had an account here for many years," he said. But since they wanted to take the dress with them, there would have to be some identification in addition to the check. Surely Mr. Farrington must have some means of identification? It was the first time Dot had heard his name spoken but she did not give any indication that it seemed strange.

Miles settled the matter by paying cash for the dress, it was two hundred, twenty-five dollars. That left him ample for any sort of festive evening and, after all, he could always get more checks cashed at the club.

The saleswoman suggested that perhaps an evening coat or cape would be necessary? Of course it would, although neither Miles nor Dot had thought of it. So in the end Miles did have to identify himself but it proved simple. The bookkeeper recognized his signature and everything was very suave after that, particularly since he paid a bill contracted by Brenda and long overdue. He would have to publish a notice, he supposed, repudiating her further debts.

With the dress and coat packed in a box, they realized Dot would need slippers and stockings. They had to hurry as the shops on the Avenue were beginning to close. "It doesn't matter," Dot said; "the stores on Broadway are open late."

But Miles was quite sure she wouldn't be able to get the proper accessories on Broadway. In the end they were both so exhausted that, when they reached the hotel laden with their bundles, they decided to rest for an hour or two before starting on their gala evening. Miles hadn't slept the night before and dropped off in a very few minutes.

When he awakened, Dot was trying to walk very quietly, back and forth, in front of the mirror set in the bathroom door. She had on all her finery.

"You look just grand," Miles said and meant it.

Dot squealed. "I didn't know you was awake. Maybe I should have taken the other dress. This does make me sort of—do you really like it?"

"You look wonderful," Miles insisted.

"Jeez, I ought to for that money," she said. It was evidently weighing on her mind. "Well, I like it best, too."

Then suddenly Miles realized they had been so busy outfitting Dot, they had entirely overlooked his evening things. He'd have to go to the club and Dot could either wait for him in a taxi or he'd come back for her. Perhaps that would be better. Dot agreed it would be, since she wasn't really dressed. She had just been trying things on. She had to do lots of things—especially to her hair which was a mess.

Miles became alarmed. "Don't frizz it up," he said; "I like it much better this way. It goes very well with the dress."

"I wasn't thinking of frizzing it," she said with dignity.

When he returned in less than an hour, feeling almost ill at ease in his tails, he noticed several empty glasses on the dresser. She was always very alert and immediately realized the direction of his eyes.

"I had a few cocktails," she said, almost apologetically. "I get so nervous when you're gone."

"I'm glad you did," Miles said, annoyed that he should have been so obvious and transparent in noticing the glasses, "but you mustn't get nervous—everything is perfectly all right. Our troubles are all over."

He had stopped to buy orchids for her and they seemed to please her more than any of the other things. "I've never worn an orchid, Mike," she said. "I guess I shouldn't call you Mike any longer, should I?" she asked as he helped her with the pinning. "It sounded funny to hear them calling you Mr. Farrington."

"I wish you would go on calling me Mike—I prefer it."

"Whatever you say."

Miles felt that she might have had a little sentimental, personal feeling about the matter but apparently she thought it more important to be agreeable and let him decide.

"We're going to have dinner at the Plaza," he said, "then a show—anyone you want to see—and then a night club; I don't know which is the most popular one at the moment but I'll call George and find out."

Both at the Plaza and the night club, which they finally selected without consulting George, he met a few acquaintances but they only exchanged friendly nods, those impersonal gestures of New Yorkers who didn't remember whether five days or five years had passed since they'd last seen him. Miles realized many people must have known of his disappearance. With all his partners privy to it, there was bound to have been a leak and yet it had not become a matter of open knowledge and not a word had seeped into the newspapers. Now that he was back, however, very few people would ask any questions. There would be many theories, all of them revolving around Brenda but all of them completely erroneous.

He did not have to be ashamed of Dot's appearance and there was no occasion to introduce her to anyone that night. She was an excellent dancer and Miles had always loved to dance, although Brenda had given him very little practice. Miles realized that the Plaza probably seemed a little dull to Dot and the food, perfectly cooked and served, didn't mean a thing. But she liked the musical show he selected and the night club was the swellest place she'd ever seen. Outside of pictures, of course.

The gala evening was not altogether successful and was over at an early hour. Perhaps it was because he wasn't drinking. He knew that it's usually dull when one person drinks and the other doesn't. Occasionally during the evening he thought of the Camden saloons and the thought was not unpleasant. It gave an added fillip to the present surroundings. Camden would always color and give new values to everything he did. He tried, impersonally, to decide whether Dot was better suited to the Plaza and the night club, with its three dollar couvert, than she was to Camden saloons with five cent beer and ten cent whiskey. He couldn't decide that point. He hadn't known many women in Camden. There had been only those two unsuccessful encounters with amateur and professional whores.

In her Carnegie finery, Dot was certainly part of the night club ensemble, although her make-up and hair were still all wrong. But that could be changed and would be. As she was, some of the regular after-midnight leerers were giving her close attention. Her youth, in spite of her experiences, was apparent and attractive.

Suddenly, they realized they were convalescents and very tired. At least they blamed their boredom on that. They agreed that the gala evening would end with "to be continued" and were glad to get back to the hotel.

Miles noticed that Dot eagerly seized the gin bottle but wouldn't let him order anything to go with it. "No," she said, "I just want a little nightcap. Plain water will do."

"You didn't have a very good time, did you?" Miles asked.

She couldn't lie. "It was wonderful, Mike," she said, "but—" She let it hang there.

"The next party we have," Miles said, "will be your party, and you'll decide on everything. How will it go?"

Dot considered. "Well, I'd have dinner at a swell Chinese restaurant; I love their expensive dinners with bird's nest soup and everything—and then I'd rather go to Radio City, I think. I don't know, but them other theatres seem so small and cheap to me. Or maybe you could get tickets to a Rudy Vallee broadcast—gee, that'd be won'erful, and then I'd like to go to Roseland and after that, if there's still life in the bodies, Harlem is my dish—y'ever been to the Cotton Club, Mike?—"

She was very carefully removing all her new-bought finery.

Miles took a deep breath. "It does sound wonderful," he said. "And I'm sure I can get tickets for the broadcast. We'll do it tomorrow night—or in a few days—just as soon as we get settled."

But somehow they didn't get around to that particular party.

The next day, the Madison Avenue beauty shop (Brenda's, of course) worked wonders as Miles knew they would. They skillfully told Dot she was the Janet Gaynor or Ann Harding type; not at all Joan Crawford or Harlow. Dot was delighted; so long as she was the type of some picture star, it was all right.

The reddish tinge was completely removed from her hair and the softest blonde shade substituted—neither platinum nor gold. Ann Harding ash, they assured her. Make-up was subdued by many degrees; eyebrows were pasted on the bald spots where Dot's tweezers had done such devastating work, and the lashes were curled and tinted. The ox-blood was ruthlessly removed from her fingernails and a modest polish substituted and there she was—ready for the next job: apartment hunting.

Miles was going to take a room at the club and she was to select her own apartment, he told her, but in the end she had nothing to do with the choice, of course. She thought Greenwich Village would be nice but Miles was against that on general principles and Dot assured him it didn't make any difference. She just happened to know a nice girl who had once lived on Barrow Street.

There was only one thing she was stubborn about. She wasn't going to let him pay an extravagant rent. She just couldn't be happy if she knew she was living in an apartment that cost enough in rent to support an entire family. Miles pointed out that the families of the men who owned the luxurious apartments wouldn't eat if their suites weren't rented but Dot refused to be sorry for them. Let them live in them and open whore houses of their own. Apparently, that was the only business Dot could think of which might pay the rent.

Eventually they took a duplex in a remodeled house on Murray Hill. Miles wanted to get away from the tyranny of doormen and elevator boys. He had suffered under them for years. Managing to get a minute alone with the agent of the building, Miles told him to halve the rent when Dot asked the figure. Not until he had signed the lease, did Dot discover she would have to walk three blocks to buy a loaf of bread and a bottle of milk. "It just shows," she said, "you can't think of everything."

Another objection was that the apartment was very inconvenient to the subway. Miles explained again that she was not to use the subway. She should take a taxi for everything until he arranged for a car and a chauffeur. He realized that the question of servants was going to be difficult. He didn't see how he was going to keep Dot from fraternizing with them. The thing would have to be done gradually. A cleaning woman at first and they would take most of their meals out. Then, after a while, as Dot learned to handle servants, others would be introduced.

Dot insisted a cleaning woman was all the household help she wanted; if she didn't have something to do, she'd go nuts. It was easy to see that she was getting lonely. She had one grief concerning which she wept a great deal. They could never have any children. After her last operation, the one which almost ended fatally, the doctors had told her she could never be a mother.

Miles consoled her—somewhat insincerely. He had no paternal urge at all. He was sure they would be happier just with each other. It sounded very hollow. He was afraid that Dot might suggest the eventual adoption of a child but apparently that hadn't occurred to her—yet. Miles had thought of himself and Dot, in Philadelphia, as a couple of waifs and strays, bound together by outlawry from the rest of the world. And now he found himself the perfectly conventional rich man with a vulgar mistress. He had known many men in similar positions and he had never envied them.

He urged her to look up some of her old friends but she refused to consider the suggestion. The friends she had didn't belong in a Murray Hill duplex and whether she knew it or not, Miles suddenly realized she didn't belong there either.

He couldn't be with her in the daytime, he had thrown himself into the business with great energy though it bored him almost beyond endurance. He was sure he would not be able to keep up the office grind indefinitely but, for the time being, he felt under great obligations to George and his other partners.

After the first few weeks, he didn't spend every evening with her. His life with Brenda had forced him into independent evening engagements—particularly bridge, and it was so easy to slip back into that life, especially when Dot insisted she didn't mind being alone and would go to two pictures instead of the usual one.

Miles noticed that she was again appearing in vulgar clothes; clothes which certainly were not purchased east of Fifth Avenue. Her hair had gone back to its copperish red. He mentioned it in a light, jocular way. Dot sulked. "To hell with Ann Harding," she said. "I like to be natural." Miles doubted if she remembered what the natural color of her hair had been but, of course, he let the matter drop.

He realized it was going to be impossible for them to have any mutual social life. He tried to make up for his neglect by giving her a huge allowance—more money than was good for her and he knew it. At first she protested and then, she said she had opened a savings bank account and became almost greedy. She had no outlet for money except for personal adornment and her purchases became more and more startling and cheap and extraordinary. Miles had never realized the full meaning of the expression "all dressed up like a Christmas tree" until Dot appeared one night sprinkled from hair to hem with rhinestone stars of generous proportions. She had copied it from a picture, she admitted, and it looked a little different!

However, since he allowed her to select their dining places and amusements when they were together, he was sure he would never meet any of his intimates. One night—it was the first time they had been out together in more than a week—they were having dinner in one of her favorite Greenwich Village places. Dinner was a dollar and a quarter with a cocktail. Miles was sure he would eventually succumb to acute indigestion but then he would remember Camden and realize that his stomach was not such a delicate, dainty organ after all. Camden always restored his perspective.

She leaned across the table to take his cocktail since he was still refusing them, which was another reason for patronizing this place. She got two free cocktails. "When will your wife get her divorce?" she asked, reaching for the olive in her glass.

"I don't know," Miles said; "any day, now, I imagine."

"Dear," she whispered, "I wonder if you would mind if I have my mother come on for our wedding; it would be the happiest day in her life."

Miles did not look at her. He did not dare. He was sure she was not intentionally blackmailing him. She apparently could not believe that a man would spend so much money on any woman except a wife or an intended wife. She was just a clinging vine and, since she knew he had been faithful to Brenda, she naturally supposed he would want to marry again immediately. With her accurate instincts, she also probably knew that he had been true to her and that on the nights he was not with her, he really was playing bridge and going to concerts, which bored her.

"Of course your mother can come on, dear," he said. "Where is she?"

"Baltimore; I told you. And if we could keep it from her, I'd rather she wouldn't know you've been divorced. She's terribly old-fashioned."

Miles could see that the old-fashioned mother-in-law would probably come to live with her daughter and rich son-in-law. And he could not object. Pliable as Dot was, she had the upper hand and some day that would become a heavy hand. She would never actually blackmail him but she would have her own indolent, vulgar way about the things that mattered to her.

Looking at her pretty, weak face, he suddenly realized there would only be one way to get rid of her. Eventually he would have to kill her. His second murder. Perhaps he would not be able to get away with it. It would not be as easy as the first time; such luck could not be repeated. But whether he could get away with it or not, he would have to do it. It was the only way he would be able to free himself from the first murder.

The idea was not unpleasant. In fact, it was the most stimulating thought that had come into his mind since Dot had returned from her newspaper reading at the library and he had learned there was nothing to fear.

In a way, Dot was not unlike Lucy, the street waif. They both had the same nervous, childlike quality. It was something more than the fact that they were both morons. Lucy had first irritated him; had probably aroused the first murderous instinct in him when she took it for granted that their relations were going to be prolonged. He remembered her exact words: "Will you buy me some clothes in the morning, daddy?" And now Dot had signed her death warrant with, "Would you mind if my mother came on to our wedding?"

"A penny for your thoughts, dear," she said with a giggle.

"They'd be worth a penny to you," he said gravely. "Do you know, dear," he said suddenly, "I think I'll have a drink."

He motioned to the waiter.

"I wish you would, Mike," she said heartily. "It gets sort of discouraging drinking alone."

"Rye," Miles said to the waiter.

"Bonded?" the waiter suggested.

"No, blended."

The waiter was contemptuous. All dolled up in tails and ordering blended ryes! But that waiter really knew nothing about blended ryes. He had never been to Camden.

Miles drank the rye without being conscious of the taste of it. He was planning a murder and it was exciting. That was the one thing which had kept his first murder from being the perfect crime. It hadn't been planned.

Alan Williams Bibliography
(1890–1945)

Novels
Free to Live (1934), William Godwin, Inc.
Holiday Madness (1934), William Godwin, Inc.
Tear Stains (1935), as Peter Marsh, Arcadia House
The Night Must End (1935), William Godwin, Inc.
Love Never Sleeps (1935), William Godwin, Inc.
Room Service (1936), William Godwin, Inc.
The Leaves Unfold (1936) as Peter Marsh, Arcadia House
Double Standard (1938), William Godwin, Inc.
Night in Manhattan (1939), William Godwin, Inc.
The Devil's Daughter (1942), as Peter Marsh, Jonathan Swift, Inc., Lion Books (1948)

Non-Fiction
American Hurly-Burly (1937) by Earnest Southerland Bates & Alan Williams, R. M. McBride & Co.

Short Fiction
"Sables and Shoplifters" *Breezy Stories* April 1922
"Gertie of the Gee Gees" *Breezy Stories* September 1922
"Night of Disillusion" *Yellow Book* #44, 1923
"Tattoo" *Breezy Stories* January 1923
"Mexican Sauce" *Young's Realistic Stories Magazine* February 1923
"No Fool Like an Old One" *Breezy Stories* February 1923
"Burgundy to Bichloride" *Young's Realistic Stories Magazine* March 1923
"The Knight of the Bath" *Droll Stories* March 1923
"The Greenwich Village Mystery" (as L. W. Lowenthal) *Top-Notch Magazine* April 1, 1923
"A Marriage under the Double Cross" *Breezy Stories* April 1923

"Mr. Spiffkin's Point of View" *Saucy Stories* April 1, 1923
"Starched Skirts" *Saucy Stories* May 15, 1923
"The Room in the Tree-Tops" *Live Stories* May 2, 1923
"A Hard-Boiled Baby" *Breezy Stories* June 1923
"Kitty Café" *Droll Stories* June 1923
"Enigma" *Saucy Stories* June 1, 1923
"Chinese Needlework" *Saucy Stories* June 15, 1923
"Don't Waste Your Sympathy" *Droll Stories* July 1923
"Great Moments and Long Years" *Breezy Stories* July 1923
"A Clean Love Story" *Saucy Stories* July 1, 1923
"Sleeping Acquaintances" *Saucy Stories* July 15, 1923
"The Burnt Flame" *Breezy Stories* September 1923
"The Last of His Name" *Young's Realistic Stories Magazine* September 1923
"Other Men's Shoes" *Droll Stories* September 1923
"Guile" *Saucy Stories* September 15, 1923
"His Flapper Bride" *Snappy Stories* September 2, 1923
"Co-Education" *Saucy Stories* November 1, 1923
"The Charm" *Saucy Stories* November 15, 1923
"Don Juan at a House Party" *Saucy Stories* December 1, 1923
"A Good Kid" *Breezy Stories* January 1924
"Love Among the Antiques" *Droll Stories* January 1924
"Waiting for Santa Claus" *Saucy Stories* January 1, 1924
"His Wedding Eve" *Telling Tales* January 1, 1924
"Denatured" *Saucy Stories* January 15, 1924
"Mary's Man" *Saucy Stories* January 15, 1924
"Neighbors on a Park Bench" *Droll Stories* February 1924
"Towards the River" *Breezy Stories* February 1924
"Lonely Youth" *Young's Realistic Stories Magazine* March 1924
"Meal Tickets" *Droll Stories* March 1924
"Petting Preferred" *Telling Tales* March 1, 1924

"Harvest" *Breezy Stories* April 1924
"Step in and Fall Out" *Droll Stories* April 1924
"The Wife Bargain" *Saucy Stories* April 1924
"One Act of Kindness" *Saucy Stories* May 1924
"The Right to His Name" *Telling Tales* May 1, 1924
"But Love Is Not Blind" *Telling Tales* May 2 1924
"Once Is Enough" *Breezy Stories* June 1, 1924
"The Collector Calls" *Breezy Stories* June 2, 1924
"The Tired Business Woman" *Telling Tales* June 1, 1924
"Flesh and Marble" *Breezy Stories* July 2, 1924
"Larry to Olive to Fluff" *Saucy Stories* August 1924
"Stripped Souls" *Telling Tales* August 1, 1924
"Eyes of Desire" *Telling Tales* August 2, 1924
"Checkered Careers" *Breezy Stories* October, 1 1924
"To the Pure" *Droll Stories* November 1924
"Men Are Like That!" *Breezy Stories* November, 1 1924
"Just His Girl" *Breezy Stories* November 2, 1924
"Bright Light Love" *Snappy Stories* November 2, 1924
"Weeping Wives" *Young's Realistic Stories Magazine* December 1924
"In Her Arms" *Breezy Stories* December 1, 1924
"Sweet and Rough" *Breezy Stories* December 2, 1924
"High Spots" *Telling Tales* December 1, 1924
"Renunciation" *Snappy Stories* December 2, 1924
"The Dancer at Dolodino's" *Snappy Stories* January 2, 1925
"Lovers of Luxury" *Breezy Stories* February 1, 1925
"Monotony—and Then—" *Breezy Stories* February 2, 1925
"Honeymoon for One" *Telling Tales* February 2, 1925
"The Color of Shame" *Breezy Stories* March 2, 1925
"The Opened Door" *Telling Tales* March 2, 1925
"Desire of the Dance Halls" *Breezy Stories* April 1, 1925
"The Lure of the Worthless" *Breezy Stories* April 2, 1925
"Out of the Ashcan" *Telling Tales* April 2, 1925

"A Dumb Way Out" *Breezy Stories* May 1, 1925
"Money's Worth" *Breezy Stories* May 2, 1925
"The Bright Vision" *Young's Realistic Stories Magazine* June 1925
"Remembered Nights" *Telling Tales* June 1925
"Sweetness and Light" *Droll Stories* July 1925
"Candy and Flowers" *Breezy Stories* July 1, 1925
"Women of Broadway" *Snappy Stories* July 1, 1925
"Three's a Crowd" *Droll Stories* August 1925
"The Cabaret Cook" *Telling Tales* September 1925
"One Indiscretion" *Droll Stories* September 1925
"Fearsome Love" *Breezy Stories* September 1, 1925
"What Does Experience Teach?" *Breezy Stories* September 2, 1925
"Right off the Griddle" *Droll Stories* October 1925
"These Charming Husbands" *Snappy Stories* October 1, 1925
"The Game Plays Out" *Droll Stories* November 1925
"—Except Love" *Breezy Stories* November 1, 1925
"Frayed Edges" *Droll Stories* December 1925
"Pirate Blood" *Breezy Stories* December 1, 1925
"This Minute's Mama" *Snappy Stories* December 1, 1925
"Neither Love nor Beauty" *Breezy Stories* December 2, 1925
"Monday to Saturday" *Droll Stories* January 1926
"Release" *Breezy Stories* January 1, 1926
"Bacchanal" *Breezy Stories* January 2, 1926
"It's a Long Way to Montclair" *Droll Stories* February 1926
"Love Among the Oranges" *Breezy Stories* February 1, 1926
"Outside the Window" *Breezy Stories* February 2, 1926
"No Mother to Guide Him" *Droll Stories* March 1926
"Return" *Breezy Stories* March 1, 1926
"The Cold Gray Dawn" *Breezy Stories* March 2, 1926

"Some Learn" *Breezy Stories* April 1, 1926
"Chameleon" *Breezy Stories* April 2, 1926
"Curtain" *Mystery Magazine* May 1, 1926
"Bright Lights and Dim" *Breezy Stories* May 1, 1926
"Stepping Out Mamas" *Snappy Stories* May 1, 1926
"The Greatest Love" *Breezy Stories* May 2, 1926
"A Sense of Security" *Droll Stories* June 1926
"Letters Home" *Snappy Stories* June 1, 1926
"The Happy Ending" *Breezy Stories* June 2, 1926
"A Bit of a Bum" *Breezy Stories* July 1926
"Murder in His Heart" *Droll Stories* July 1926
"Thanks for the Buggy Ride" *Droll Stories* August 1926
"Hearts and Harems" *Young's Realistic Stories Magazine* September 1926
"Sex-Appeal Sally" *Droll Stories* September 1926
"Kiernan the Killer" *Adventure* September 23, 1926
"An Arizona Aristocrat" *Adventure* October 8, 1926
"The Pact" *Young's Realistic Stories Magazine* October 1926
"Payment Demanded" *Breezy Stories* October 1926
"Dollar Dazed" *Young's Realistic Stories Magazine* November 1926
"Rena Reduces" *Droll Stories* November 1926
"No More Bare Knees" *Droll Stories* December 1926
"No Sentiment—Allowed" *Breezy Stories* December 1926
"Portrait of a Flirt" *Young's Realistic Stories Magazine* December 1926
"Mistakes" *Breezy Stories* January 1927
"The Pure Youth" *Droll Stories* January 1927
"The Virtuous Type" *Young's Realistic Stories Magazine* January 1927
"It Was the Cat" *Droll Stories* February 1927
"The Price of Genius" *Young's Realistic Stories Magazine* February 1927
"Unafraid" *Breezy Stories* February 1927

"Certain Reservations" *Young's Realistic Stories Magazine* March 1927

"The Revolt of the Typewriter" *Snappy Stories* March 1927

"Somebody's Son" *Droll Stories* March 1927

"Betty's Background" *Droll Stories* April 1927

"Matinées" *Breezy Stories* April 1927

"Time's Changes" *Young's Realistic Stories Magazine* April 1927

"License" *Breezy Stories* May 1927

"The Long Years" *Young's Realistic Stories Magazine* June 1927

"Night-Club Charlie" *Droll Stories* June 1927

"Pa and Ma" *Breezy Stories* June 1927

"Beside a Babbling Brook" *Young's Realistic Stories Magazine* July 1927

"Mixed Morals" *Breezy Stories* July 1927

"The Golden Key" *Breezy Stories* August 1927

"Setting" *Young's Realistic Stories Magazine* August 1927

"Broadway Faces" *Breezy Stories* September 1927

"What the Burglar Wanted" *Young's Realistic Stories Magazine* September 1927

"The One-Woman Idea" *Young's Realistic Stories Magazine* October 1927

"To Keep the Faith" *Breezy Stories* October 1927

"Daughters" *Young's Realistic Stories Magazine* November 1927

"Doubtful Value" *Breezy Stories* November 1927

"Unoriginal Sinners" *Young's Realistic Stories Magazine* December 1927

"E.E.E." *Sweetheart Stories* #64, December 13, 1927

"The Price of a Frock" *Breezy Stories* January 1928

"Two on a Modern Tower" *Young's Realistic Stories Magazine* January 1928

"The Blame" *Young's Realistic Stories Magazine* February 1928

"Annulment" *Young's Realistic Stories Magazine* March 1928

"Financing Folly" *Breezy Stories* March 1928

"That Terrible Woman" *Young's Realistic Stories Magazine* June 1928

"The Middle of the Night" *Young's Realistic Stories Magazine* July 1928

"The Frock of Fate" *Young's Realistic Stories Magazine* August 1928

"Webbing" *Breezy Stories* March 1929

"Shopping" *Breezy Stories* July 1929

"Women of Wall Street" *Breezy Stories* October 1929

"Letty's a Lady Now" *Breezy Stories* December 1929

"Sheep" *Breezy Stories* January 1930

"Aftermath" *Young's Magazine Snappy Stories* February 1930

"Pastoral" *Breezy Stories* March 1930

"This Little Girl" *Breezy Stories* June 1931

"Love-Affair" *Breezy Stories* August 1931

"Things We Want Most" *Breezy Stories* September 1931

"Dudes and Diamonds" *Western Romances* #19, October 1931

"The Clutch of the Past" *Sweetheart Stories* #180, January 12, 1932

"Angels Should Not Marry" (with Alton Cook) *Breezy Stories* September 1933

"Lovers Come Back" *Breezy Stories and Young's Magazine* February 1934

"—But Always" *Breezy Stories and Young's Magazine* March 1934

"Sweethearts Forever" *Thrilling Love* March 1934

"Passionate Broadcast" *Breezy Stories* and *Young's Magazine* May 1934

"The Perfect Stranger" *Breezy Stories* and *Young's Magazine* August 1934

"Tropical Fragrance" *Breezy Stories* and *Young's Magazine* June 1935

"Lie in the Sun" *Breezy Stories* and *Young's Magazine* July 1935

"Something New for Reno" *Breezy Stories* August 1935

"Thawing Out" *Breezy Stories* September 1935

"For Insurance Salesmen" *Breezy Stories* October 1935

"Key West Mae" *The Elks Magazine* October 1935

"In the Middle of the Day" *Breezy Stories* November 1935

"Amateur" *Breezy Stories* December 1935

"An Amazing Thing" *Breezy Stories* January 1936

"Day-Coach" *Breezy Stories* March 1936

"Vindicated" *Breezy Stories* April 1936

"Difficulties of Divorce" *Breezy Stories* July 1936

"Heart-Beats" *Breezy Stories* September 1936

"Yellow" *Breezy Stories* October 1936

"Sing Me to Sleep" *Breezy Stories* and *Young's Magazine* January 1937

"Afternoon Record" *Breezy Stories* and *Young's Magazine* February 1937

"Home—Via Reno" *Breezy Stories* and *Young's Magazine* March 1937

"The Hounds of Hollywood" *Breezy Stories* and *Young's Magazine* June 1937

"No Second Chance" *Breezy Stories* and *Young's Magazine* July 1937

"No Fury" *Breezy Stories* and *Young's Magazine* August 1937

"Non-Fiction Affection" *Breezy Stories* and *Young's Magazine* January 1938

"Head Man's Girl" *Breezy Stories* and *Young's Magazine* April 1939

"Blind Bowboy Delayed" *Breezy Stories* April 1940
"On Her Own" *Breezy Stories* April 1945
"Night After Night" *Breezy Stories* June 1945
"Ashes of Burned Out Flames" *Breezy Stories* February 1946

Noir classics from

Bodies Are Dust P. J. Wolfson
"Plenty of hard edged banter, muscular prose and clever riffing on jazz melancholy in this cruel and poignant tale . . . despair that rings so true it hurts."

—Paul Burke, *Crime Time*

I Was a Bandit Eddie Guerin
"Colorful language keeps the pages turning . . . True crime fans will welcome this memoir by a forgotten but once famous criminal."
—*Publishers Weekly*

Round Trip/Criss-Cross Don Tracy
" . . . you won't be disappointed. A tour de force of noir magic."
—Larque Press

Grimhaven Robert Joyce Tasker
"A notable, a keen and intensely moving account of what happens to a man in prison . . ."

—*New York World*

Fully Dressed and in His Right Mind Michael Fessier
"It's one of those books that can affect readers in so many different ways . . . I found it sublimely mysterious and fantastically satisfying."
—J. F. Norris, *Pretty Sinister Books*

How to Commit a Murder Danny Ahearn
" . . . a truly dangerous book . . ."

—*Lansing State Journal*

Fiction and true crime from the Jazz Age—only $12.99 each.

Stark House Press, 1315 H Street, Eureka, CA 95501
Available from your local bookstore, or order direct via our website—
www.starkhousepress.com.

www.ingramcontent.com/pod-product-compliance
Lightning Source LLC
LaVergne TN
LVHW010217070526
838199LV00062B/4625